These Bodies

by

Morgan Christie

Tolsun Books
Flagstaff, Arizona & Las Vegas, Nevada

Edited by David Pischke.

Cover art by Morgan Christie.
Set in Book Antiqua 11pt font. Design by David Pischke.

These stories first appeared in slightly varied form in the following publications: "The Panther," *Little Patuxent Review*; "Cromartie Street," *BLF Press*; "12 Steps," *Obra/Artifact*; "Dry Dreams," *Canada Quarterly*; "The Stranger," *Thrice Publishing*; "Sonic Boom," *Santa Fe Writers Project*.

ISBN 978-1-948800-36-5

Published by Tolsun Books, an imprint of Tolsun Publishing, Inc. Flagstaff, Arizona & Las Vegas, Nevada.
www.tolsunbooks.com

For my sister, Jamie —
for showing me all that love can be

Contents

These Bodies

The Panther

Keisha's pregnancy was difficult. There was a time she swore the baby churned in her womb. He wouldn't stop spinning, sloshing around like a fish washed up on a pier somewhere she'd never visited. Her stomach was undulating and there was no explanation other than the child. They found out it was boy at the five-month mark, not long after she realized she was pregnant. She'd go months without her period sometimes, usually during training. Her mother said it was normal, happened to her all the time when she was running hurdles.

"That was a real event," her mother would say. "Not like you pansy-asses that just run from point A to B."

Keisha was due in a few weeks and was still vomiting. Her doctor said it was rare but could happen, a hormonal imbalance that affected digestion throughout. She'd have to relax as much as possible to retain her energy and attend weekly appointments. Which was where she and her mother were headed. Not right away, they had a stop to make first.

Keisha's mother stepped on the brakes without warning, forcing her daughter's stomach and chest forward into the seat belt. Keisha almost said "Ouch," but didn't bother. Her mother leaned on the horn for longer than she should have before Marques came running outside. He still had his joggers on, so was probably just getting home from practice. He got in the back seat.

"Sorry I took so long," Marques said.

"Hmm," Keisha's mother replied.

Marques whispered to Keisha, "How you feelin'?"

"Fine," Keisha said, then nodded.

The car ride was mostly quiet. Her mother turned on the radio to drown it out, and they listened to the oldies station. Keisha hated Motown. Not because it was bad, but because it was all her mother played. She knew the names of more artists from the '60s and '70s then she did modern ones. A few times, Keisha listened to the radio at track practice, during warm up. The newer stuff was so intense, heavy beats and rapid rhythms, something you could run to. Keisha liked it. She'd get Marques to let her listen to his iPod any chance she got. She asked her mother for one once, an iPod. She was met with what she expected: sure, go get yourself one. It was the ethic of the house, Keisha could have anything she wanted, if she could buy it herself. So she found a job and had almost saved up enough for the iPod. Keisha was completely oblivious to the fact that she'd need a laptop to download the music onto before uploading it to the device. That money went towards the laptop instead. So she kept working, right up the street at the local grocer. Scanning bottles and cans, and ringing up chicken and bananas – until she was told to relax, of course. Until her spinning boy became reckless, too out of control for her to manage.

Keisha's mother pressed hard on the brakes, again.

"Ya'll are going to have to take the bus back," Keisha's mother said.

"But the doctor said-" Keisha began to speak.

"But nothing," her mother interrupted. "Tell the doctor to give you a ride home then. One of us has to work."

Keisha wanted to interject but Marques spoke first, "I'll get her home."

They got out of the car and signed in at the front

desk. Keisha hated the waiting room. Pictures of red, blue, and yellow ABC blocks with parenting and pregnancy magazines scattered over tables like nothing else existed. She mostly hated it there because of Marques, because he was always with her. He never missed an appointment, not once in the nearly four months she'd been going. He was supportive. He'd check on her every night, call her in the morning, and go out of his way to walk her from class to class, even if he was late for his own. Keisha's mother said it was uncommon behavior for a seventeen-year-old.

"It balances out though, doesn't it," she said some months ago. "He's responsible now, but had the two of you been responsible in the first place, you wouldn't be in this mess."

She was right of course. Small pieces of Keisha wished he was a deadbeat. That he never called, avoided her at school, tried to convince her to abort the baby, anything. If he had been a deadbeat, she'd have a reason to be angry with him, but Marques was elated when she told him the news. Even more so when he found out it was a boy. He wanted to name him after himself. Keisha wasn't sure. She found it egotistical and limiting, but she didn't care enough to put up a fight. She figured he'd been so good about everything, he deserved it.

The nurse came out and called them to the back where she admitted all the precursory to-dos before the doctor came.

"You feeling alright, Keisha?" the doctor asked as she motioned for Keisha to lay back.

Keisha nodded and the doctor put her hands against Keisha's belly. She always flinched just before the doctor's hands made contact, out of fear that they'd be cold, but they never were. They were warm and soft and gentle, though firm. Keisha often wanted to ask what she was looking for. Instead she would just imitate the same pressings in the privacy of her own room. She'd press and for a moment the baby would seem to be still, she would press harder and then he would too. She wasn't sure if it was a foot or fist, but a small bump would slowly grow against where she pressed and she knew it was him, pushing back.

The doctor loaded Keisha's stomach up with ultrasound gel and began the swirls. It tickled a bit, she told Marques once, after that every time the ultrasound began he'd glance at her and smile. Sometimes she would take his hand.

"There he is," the doctor said. "Growing like a weed, this one. Looks like he'll be here any day."

Keisha's eyes began to wander away from the screen. There were only so many times she could look at what was soon to be. She realized how bright the room was, blinding almost. She couldn't believe she'd never noticed it. White light, white walls, white counters, white cabinets. She felt the baby roll then, harshly.

"Did you see that?" Marques asked, excitedly.

"I'm sure she felt it!" the doctor responded.

Keisha asked, "Why does he move around so much?"

The doctor shrugged, "Some babies just do."

She wiped Keisha's belly and told her to keep relaxing. That it'd all be over soon, and before she knew it, he'd be here. The bus stop wasn't far from the doctor's office and the bus arrived moments after Keisha and Marques got there. He paid her bus fare and the two sat in the first pair of double seats. Keisha looked out the window and imagined having a stroller beside her, with a different Marques there. She looked out the window and wondered if she'd still be looking out the window when the little Marques was next to her, or if she'd be looking at him.

"You feeling okay today?" Marques asked.

"Mhmm," Keisha mumbled.

He touched the back side of her hand, "You seem kinda far away..."

Keisha looked at him, "I'm just tired. But can I ask you something?"

Marques nodded.

"I never thought about asking because everyone said I should be grateful," Keisha said as she faced him. "But, why were so happy when I told you? About the baby…"

Marques paused a moment then shrugged, "I just was."

Keisha frowned slightly and he noticed, so he elaborated.

"I mean, we only did it one time," Marques whispered. "It's like, it was meant to be or something."

Keisha turned back towards the window and shut her eyes. It was exactly the type of comment she figured he'd make. Surface level and not thought out. She wanted to say, *Meant to be? For who? You? Cus' it damn sure ain't me!* Her mother warned her of these feelings though, of the anger she'd have towards Marques one day. He wouldn't have to leave school, or quit track, or be up ten times a night. He wouldn't have to carry a load around for the world to gawk at or judge. He wouldn't be another teenage mother raising a child while the father went on with his life, and that wasn't his fault. Keisha opened her eyes and saw that her stop was coming up. Marques prepared to get off the bus with her.

"No," Keisha said. "I'll be fine."

"But I told your mom-"

"And I'm telling you, I'll be fine," she said. "I just want to be alone."

Keisha walked off the bus, not looking back at Marques, and she saw the grocery store on the next block. She hadn't gone back in there since she left a month before, by doctor's orders. She started heading for the store and questioned herself every step of the way. She didn't have any money, wasn't craving anything, but her brain had completely taken hold of the idea of walking into the grocery store. So she did. She picked up a basket, purely out of instinct, and glanced at her old register. Number seven. There was a red-headed woman she'd never seen there before. Popping gum and speeding through food like she'd been doing it her whole life. She looked old, Keisha could tell she wasn't, but she looked it. Probably in her late thirties early forties, but she had deep crow's feet, like the bird nested near her eyes for a season or two. Too many laugh lines as well, Keisha thought it strange, as she looked like the type of person who rarely laughed.

"Keisha?" she heard a voice call from behind her. "Oh my god, it's so good to see you!"

The assistant manager got in front of her before she could turn around.

"How have you been? Aren't you due soon?

We've missed you. You wouldn't believe all the-"

Keisha nodded, a lot. She never could get in a word edgewise with the woman, but she was happy for it that day. She slid away after another few minutes and began weaving the aisles, avoiding ex-coworkers. Until she ended up in aisle twelve, and he was there. Stocking the shelves with what looked to be boxes of cookies or granola bars. She started walking towards him the way she did when she saw the grocery store after coming off the bus. Questioning herself the entire way. She had no idea what she would say, but her brain took hold of the idea again, and she couldn't stop.

"Hey," Keisha said.

Mr. Stein looked at her and she saw his heart sink. Right there on his uniform beside the clip on tie. It was the first time the two came face to face since before he started avoiding her four months ago. He'd avoid the registers like they were contagious and duck and dodge through the aisles when she was on the floor. When he did have to be around her, staff meetings and price checks, he'd never look at her. Over or around, sure, but never at her. Not until today, today Keisha would be seen. Today he had to look.

"Keisha," Mr. Stein said. "How are you?"

"About as good as you'd imagine…"

He didn't respond, just looked down at the

dolly of what Keisha could now see were piles of cookie boxes. He had more grey hair since she'd seen him last and his liver spots seemed more pronounced. She was sure they weren't, but they seemed to be. His beer belly was protruded and his wrinkled anchor tattoo was still partially showing under his three-quarter sleeve. She was the only one that knew what it was. The other workers had a running joke about the tattoo's identity, only being able to see the bottom of it. An arrow, upside down, aluminate, triangle, heart, ice cream cone, etc, but Keisha knew, and never told. He was nice sometimes, before she told him. "Listen carefully," he'd say, or "let me help you". Then he'd show her how to do things she already knew how to do; like ring up an item that wouldn't scan, or how to best stack cans of soup, or lug stock from the storage freezer, or help her clean up when the rest of the staff was gone. And sometimes he'd show her things she didn't know how to do. She'd let him. It seemed important to him, and she knew if she didn't he'd find somebody else that would. When word got around that she was pregnant, all that stopped. She almost wished he'd look at her the same way everyone else did, like some broken thing. But he refused.

"Why are you here?" he finally asked.

The question caught Keisha off guard. She

wasn't sure, but she said the first thing that came to mind.

"I want an iPod," she said.

"Excuse me?"

"An iPod!" Keisha went on. "I saved up enough for a laptop but not for the iPod."

He only stared at her.

"You know how important it is to me," she said, louder than she intended to.

Mr. Stein stepped towards her, lifting his hands up with his palms down, "Shhh."

Keisha stepped back and Mr. Stein stopped his approach.

"Okay," he said. "I'll get it. But you need to leave."

"Why?" she asked.

The two stood in the empty aisle, stuck in the store's busy hum. Noises surrounded them like a swarm of gnats, filling their nostrils and ears and attempting to penetrate their mouths. Neither would let them, their mouth firmly shut and eyes glued to the other. Keisha wanted to scream. Nothing audible, she just wanted to make noise. To let the gnats consume her body and join in with the terrible sounding swarm around her. But she walked away. As quickly as her sore feet would let her. Two employees she knew tried to speak but she kept going. She kept going until she got home and laid down on her twin bed. She was more tired than angry, the boy spinning inside her like he was possessed. Keisha felt like she was going to be sick, and like she was going to fall asleep, and like she was going to throw herself down the stairs all at the same time. She looked at her cellphone, it had been on silent. She missed a call from Marques. Her eyes were becoming heavy. She thought about calling him. So heavy. She opened her text messages instead. She barely had the strength to type her message, but she managed to moments before her eyes closed.

I'm not ready for this.

Keisha is laying on the conveyor belt at her cashier station, naked. "What the hell?" she whispers while on her back with her legs open. There is a Nat Geo magazine next to her head with a baby panther and a baby zebra on the front cover. She takes notice before she notices him.

Mr. Stein runs up and tells her everything will be alright and takes his hand and places it on her belly button. He smiles at her, and then forces his palm downward into her stomach. The pain is severe. Keisha attempts to push his hand away, but she realizes that she cannot move.

"Listen carefully," Mr. Stein says. "They are

going to tell you to push, you have to resist. What-ever you do, Keisha, do not push."

He disappears as quickly as he came, and then her mother and Marques are there. Both beside her standing next to the conveyor belt. "Listen well, baby," the mother says. Marques interrupts, "When we say *push*, wait, and only push when we say *push harder*. Okay?" They sound like each other, her mother and her lover, they continue to speak as though they have been possessed by the other. "Okay," Marques repeats himself. Keisha attempts to nod, forgetting she cannot move, and says, "Alright."

Suddenly, music begins to play on the over-head speakers. The song is deafening, but it is a song that Keisha knows. Her mother would sometimes play it: *If You Don't Know Me By Now*, by the Blue Notes. The song is not playing all the way through, only the chorus, as if on repeat or the audio player is defective, or defiant.

The store doors slide open and Mr. Stein has returned, and he says nothing this time. He only stands in the background but is in Keisha's line of sight. Her mother coaches, "Breathe, sweetheart," and continues to speak. Keisha cannot hear her over the music. Soon, all she sees are her moth-er's lips mouthing the same shapes over and over, and Marques nodding. "I can't hear you," Keisha yells. Marques shouts, "Push!" Keisha begins to push, and Marques slaps her belly. Keisha wants scream, it hurt more than she expected it to, but instead she just looks at Mr. Stein. Marques shouts again, "Push, harder!" She is still looking at Mr. Stein, he pulls an Oreo cookie from his pocket and crumbles it between his fingers. "You have to push harder, Keisha," her mother says loudly. Marques agrees, "Push from the balls of your feet, do it!" Mr. Stein finally speaks, "Too late…"

Marques leans in close, "Put your weight under your feet, and feel the impulse. You have to push harder." Keisha lifts her hips off the conveyor and it begins to move, her mother touches the side of her face, her hand is cold and hard. Her mother opens her mouth to speak, but Keisha still cannot hear her, she only hears the chorus… *If you don't know me by now.* Keisha lowers her hips and the music stops.

She blinks and she finds herself on the track, still naked, in the seventh lane. She begins to run, passing rows of dusty red arena seats. Her mother is waiting at the finish line, holding a clipboard, noting her daughters form and what needs to be corrected once she crosses the line. Keisha is almost out of track, and her mother's face is clear now, she is neither smiling nor frowning. She is simply waiting. Keisha hears the Blue Notes again, this time coming from the loud speakers. Her strides slow to the beat of the song, and she spins arounds and starts running the other way. Keisha feels like a runner again, not the daughter of a once hurdler, but a runner. She feels her body, kinetic and sweaty, as the once empty seats begin to fill. The crowd sits with their mouths wide, like stalks of slanted wheat watching her round naked body fly by. Somewhere inside, Keisha feels astonishing. Not fast or athletic or pregnant, astonishing. All eyes are on her and her stomach churns again, but the churns turn to light. She is glowing, her stomach is glowing. Maybe there is no baby, maybe it's just light, but then why would they tell her to...

"Push harder," Marques screams now. Keisha is on the conveyor belt again and she is pushing, but nothing is coming out. Mr. Stein walks towards the three of them now and stands by Keisha's feet. He lifts his Oreo crumb-ridden hands upward and slowly enters Keisha. "I'm just trying to help you," Mr. Stein says. Keisha screams but the Blue Notes' song comes out instead. She tries to close her legs but forgets she can't move. So she pushes, harder. Her stomach spinning and the child resisting. She glances at the Nat Geo magazine again, the animals are no longer babies. They are fully grown, the panther and the zebra; but the zebra is not acting like prey, nor is the panther acting like a predator. They just are. Keisha feels Mr. Stein's hands pulling out of her, and with it the spinning sensation. He's pulling it out of her; her mother and Marques watch, but soon Keisha feels nothing. She closes her eyes and feels her mother's hand again, just as cold and hard as the first time.

Keisha awoke to her phone lit up next to her cheek. She squinted at the crimson blue glow and its excessiveness. There were so many text messages. She was only asleep for an hour, but there were seventeen of them. All from Marques.

What do you mean?

Huh?

Of course you are.

What do you mean?

Are you there?

Keisha?

Can you talk to me please?

Did I do something wrong?

Why won't you answer?

What are you going to do?

Keisha?!?

Missed call "Ques" — 6:07pm

Answer the phone.

Please.

I'm coming over.

Five minutes away…

Outside.

Missed call "Ques" — 6:42

Are you there?

Missed call "Ques" — 6:46

It was 6:52 now. Keisha rolled out of bed and went to the intercom. She didn't ask if he was there, she just pushed the buzzer and heard the entrance click. She unlocked the door and sat down with her legs spread across the couch. Marques was coming in not even a minute later.

"What's going on?" he asked. "What do you mean you're not ready?"

"I'm not," Keisha replied. "And neither are you."

"Yes we are."

"We're kids, Marques, not even eighteen," she said. "Two kids that wanted to run track in college and get scholarships and go to prom. Now we're going to be parents. And now only one of us is getting that scholarship."

Keisha leaned back and covered her face.

"I won't go if you don't want me to," Marques said. "I'll work go work with my dad an-"

"That's not what I want," Keisha said, sitting

up straight.

Marques shrugged, "Well what then? Just tell me what you want me to do."

Keisha didn't answer. He couldn't give her what she wanted. She thought about telling him how her mother guilted her out of adoption, because she needed to own her responsibilities, not pawn them off on someone else; or the reason why Mr. Stein stopped looking at her four months ago; or that she wanted to name the baby after her father because he wasn't around, and she had hoped her son would take after him; she even thought of telling him she was terrified of being a mother, because she wasn't sure what that meant. She didn't, because what she really wanted from Marques was for him to understand how she felt. She wanted what he couldn't give her. Instead, she told him something else.

"I just had a dream about a panther and a zebra," Keisha said. "I'm a panther, and you're a panther; but what if our son isn't. What if he's more like a zebra, Marques? Spinning and turning and rolling and scared and never knowing which way to go. What if he's not like us?"

Marques looked more confused than Keisha had ever seen him look. More than when she helped him study for their calculus midterm, or their first date a year and a half ago when she told him she didn't listen to music, or when she asked him for sex for the first time a few months after she started her new job because she wanted to know how it felt when she asked for it.

"Then we'll love him anyway," Marques said before he smiled at her like he did at the doctor's office.

He said the right thing, and she was furious.

"It was all for the music, Marques," Keisha whispered. "I just wanted a thing that was mine."

CROMARTIE STREET

She'd been to six stores that hour, and not one of them had salt.

"What kind of shit is this," she muttered to herself.

Rayon was semi-new to the Bronx, and first thought it was something as simple as not knowing where to look. Until the third store, anyway. After the fifth, she started imagining it some sort of mediocre conspiracy, a bored teenager's ploy to see to it that no meal north of Manhattan would consist of any flavor. But after the sixth, it was just funny. She was shaking her head while taming a modest giggle when she saw it, lit up on the neon green street sign like it was layered in highlighter. Cromartie Street.

There was nothing peculiar about the street

name, but Rayon had been up and down that block several times, that day alone, and had not once recalled seeing a Cromartie Street. The street name didn't even show up with Google Maps, so she knew something was up. Down the road were mostly barren lots overtaken by gnarled weeds and too-bright dandelions; there were purple flowers too, small ones. Rayon had no idea what they were, just that they were small, clustered, and inviting. The little flowers surrounded the only building occupying the block — a big box of a building with white signage above the front window laced in flashing rainbow lights. The words as jarring as the sign, "SALT HERE".

Rayon almost crept up to the building, expecting some oddly finagled apparition to jump out and scare her into oblivion. There was no door, just an open space under the sign and between the windows. She stuck her head in first, surveying the shop like the whole odd occurrence was something normal. The signage didn't lie, she saw salt immediately. It was all she saw. Rows and rows of salt lining every shelf in the store. Nothing but salt, and an oversized cash register. She stepped inside and wandered over to the nearest shelf, picking up the first packet on the row. Rayon could have sworn that when she touched the salt a gust blew into the shop, knocking her high pony off to the side.

She heard the woman before she saw her, unsure of which would have caught her more off guard.

"Looking for salt," an old raspy voice echoed through the small space.

Rayon turned around and almost dropped the pack. Directly in the middle of the store stood a small stout woman, head wrapped in a tan silk scarf with matching drapery waterfalling her silhouette. Her skin looked just as Rayon's father's once looked—smooth, cool, and a rich deep seeded brown—but the woman had moles, moles that resembled freckles. They were most everywhere on her cheeks, chin, and in abundance on her forehead. The woman stepped closer to Rayon, extending her arms, motioning to the rows of product.

"Looking for salt?" she asked again.

"Oh," Rayon stuttered. "Yeah, I'll just grab this one."

The woman waddled to the register and Rayon followed down behind her. She placed the salt on the counter and the woman began to ring her up.

"Will you be needing a bag?" the woman asked.

"No," Rayon said while shaking her head. "I'm good."

The woman smiled, a beautiful smile. The kind that made the room and anyone in it light up. Rayon smiled back at her. It dawned on her that that was the first time she'd smiled that day — chasing salt was no smiling matter, even when it became laughable.

"How much is it?" Rayon asked.

The woman continued ringing her up, furiously pressing the old broken down buttons on the register.

The woman pursed her lips and gave Rayon an almost under-eyed look before she said, "It's cheap, darling, just eleven strands…"

"Sorry," Rayon replied as she leaned in, assuming she heard incorrectly.

"Eleven strands," the woman annunciated.

"Strands of what?" Rayon asked.

The woman responded, "Hair, of course. That's the currency here."

Rayon looked at the woman like she was joking, but, lo and behold, the woman's once beautiful laugh didn't reappear and all that was left was the under-eyed annoyance.

"You want me to pay you in hair?" Rayon repeated.

The woman only nodded.

Rayon touched the tip of her freshly permed

ponytail and stared at the woman staring at her.

"Is this a joke?" she questioned.

"No," the woman said. "Just the currency we take. You have plenty of hair, surely you can spare eleven strands."

The woman pulled out a pair of scissors from seemingly nowhere and slid them towards Rayon.

"You won't find salt anywhere else," the woman said lowly as she removed her hand from the scissors.

Rayon twisted her fingers over the strands, feeling each individual one roll over atop her finger and thumb prints, settling along the grooves of her identity.

"What'll it be?" the woman sounded more annoyed now.

Rayon thought of turning around and leaving the salt on the counter. Saying screw the old lady and taking off out of the store; but then she remembered the six shops, and the time, and that if she didn't put the soup on in a few hours it wouldn't be ready the next day when her mother and sister were due. Rayon rolled her eyes and pulled the elastic off the top of her head. She grabbed a small bundle of hair and began piecing out a tiny section. She started counting then, *one*, *two*, the strands were soft and sharp, *three*, *four*, like a razor or edge of paper, *five, six*, but not so sharp they could cut her, *seven, eight*, just enough to remind her that her curls were gone, *nine, ten*, that they'd been tamed, *eleven*.

Rayon put her strands of hair on the counter and the woman scooped them up in a noticeable hurry. She pushed the salt towards Rayon and stuffed her hair deep into the open register.

"Thank you, darling," the woman said, motioning for Rayon to head towards the space between the windows.

Rayon winced a bit at the woman's abruptness, but picked up her salt and left. She had some soup to start on. Rayon's walk shifted into a half jog as she hurried home. She had to get the beans on. It was her first year preparing the soup, the memorial soup if you will. It'd been eleven years and three-hundred and sixty-four days since her father's untimely demise. Rayon didn't know what killed her father, just that he didn't wake up after a nap one day. Her mother refused an autopsy, so that was that.

"He's gone," her mother said. "Cutting him open won't bring him back."

Every year on the anniversary of his death, Rayon, her mother, and sister Vy would come together for a day of remembrance and red pea soup, their father's favorite. This was Rayon's first year hosting the lunch, after years of trying to convince her mother. The last thing she needed was bland soup, a reason for her mother to never allow one of her daughters to cook for the family again.

She rushed up the stairs in her apartment building, the beat of reggaeton pulsing through the walls; she could feel the vibrations under her feet. They almost jolted her upwards and into the apartment, where she became winded, but flew into the kitchen and immediately added salt to the pot of low boiling beans on the stove. They'd stay like this overnight, before anything else would be added; the beef, peppers, and other seasonings. Only after Rayon salted the bean water did she realize her exhaustion. She'd been running around most of the afternoon in her quest for salt, and it caught up to her. Rayon began stripping down before getting into her bedroom, first her black tank and then her favorite pair of tights. She always went underwearless, save her period week, as she wore pads instead of tampons due to a horrid toxic shock event when she was seventeen. That was over ten years ago, but it felt like yesterday to Rayon. Her bare body hit the bed and she sank into the comforter. Before rolling off to sleep, Rayon ran her fingers over the small patch of pulled strands and hoped that the soup would be worth the new growth she'd be facing. Her phone rang, but she was asleep before the sound resonated with the rest of her.

Rayon is a jellyfish, swimming wrathfully in a red ocean thick with purple seaweed and stringy blue rocks that don't know they're supposed to be dense. She looks around for more of her kind in hopes of being a part of a swarm, but swarms don't exist in this ocean. So, she continues to swim and search, even though searching is futile. As she swims, she feels a pop come from her lower body, when she looks back, she sees one of her tentacles floating behind her like it belonged there. She keeps swimming. She feels three more pops, but doesn't look back. She begins to worry then. If she keeps swimming all of her tentacles may pop off, but then how will she swim? If she stops swimming then her tentacles will cease to fall off, but then how will she find the swarm? Even if it is futile. She keeps swimming, watching the stringy blue rocks pass by like they were exactly the way they were made to be.

The sun hit Rayon's back like fire on aloe—hot, sticky, and refreshing. She stood and stretched the way she did every morning, a half-formed sun salutation. Rayon felt good, not stiff and tight like she would most days after sleeping on her brick mattress. Her sun salutation wasn't so half-baked that morning... She jumped in a cold shower and washed the salty layer off her back, feeling every pore take a well-needed sigh of relief. Rayon stepped from behind the curtain and saw herself in a light she hadn't since... since... ever. She stepped closer to the mirror and put her hand on her head, feeling nothing but stubble. Her hair was gone. All of it. She began rubbing her head like it was an illusion, as though if she kept making contact her hair would suddenly reappear.

Rayon pulled the shower curtain back, no hair. She went into her room, not a strand in sight. It had just disappeared, and she was sure she knew who to blame. Rayon grabbed another pair of tights and a t-shirt before bolting out the door. She skipped about two steps at a time and took off out of the building. She was in a full sprint by time she touched the sidewalk, and she stayed that way until she neared Cromartie Street. Well, where Cromartie should have been. She looked around at the two streets paralleling the invisible Cromartie.

"What on earth?" she said as she blew.

Rayon asked a few passersby if she was in the right area, they'd never heard of the street.

"And I've lived here since '72, though they'll

try buying me out before '22!" one man exclaimed, "No Cromartie round here."

Rayon ran home and noticed how steady her breathing was, even as she climbed the multiple stories, she felt evened out. As if the air was being absorbed by the same pores that opened up that very morning. She felt reinvigorated in her angst. She got home and flopped down on her bed again.

"Damn that old Obeah woman," Rayon mumbled under her breath.

She reached for her phone and saw them, the twelve missed calls from the night before. Stacy. She knew it before checking the call log; she was the only person Rayon knew that would call that many times without sending a text. There were no messages either. Big brother and all. She might have been the only person in Rayon's life that was happy about the Snowden stuff, because it meant she was right. Rayon had known Stacy for five years; they'd been an item for three. They broke up almost a year before and attempted to stay friends with little success. She imagined the excuse this time would be the anniversary of her father's death, but if it wasn't one thing it was another. Rayon wanted the whole thing to stop. They weren't good for each other. The love was hard, and heavy and fluid, but so was everything else. The break up was Rayon's idea, and whenever she was asked what happened, there was never any definite answer...

It just was. Rayon picked up the phone and rested her finger on the call button, but she swiped it away. Cold turkey, that's what they call it.

Rayon went into the kitchen and turned up the heat on the pot; the beans had softened and the salt-water had become the same burgundy shade. She added the rest of the ingredients to the pot and stirred the soup for nearly an hour. They'd be there soon, so Rayon set the table. This would also be her mother's first time seeing her new place; Vy had been over a few times before. She moved to the Bronx as a community organizer, to live with the people she worked for on a daily basis. Her mother didn't understand it, giving up a rent controlled apartment in lower Manhattan for space in a triplex so far out of the city, but Rayon didn't expect her mother to understand, she rarely did. There was a knock on the door.

"It's open," Rayon yelled.

Her sister pushed the door open to their mother saying, "You can't be so reckless, Rayon, how on earth are you leaving the door unlocked like this?"

"Hey Ma," Rayon said as her sister joined her in the kitchen and hugged her neck.

"The hell happened to your hair," her sister Vy

asked.

Rayon rolled her eyes as she said, "Don't ask."

Their mother entered the kitchen, "Well your hair comes as no surprise to me. Isn't that the next step?"

"Next step towards what, Ma?"

The room became quiet, Vy glanced at her mother as Rayon stared at her. Their mother sat down and motioned to her empty bowl.

"Soup..." their mother said.

Vy sat down next to her and Rayon began to share out the food. Their bowls were filled to the brim and Rayon joined them at the table. They didn't say grace on this day — the only day their mother didn't say grace — as their father didn't care much for religion. They sipped the soup, and remembered.

"It's good Ray," Vy said.

Rayon smiled at her sister, "Thanks. What do you think, Ma?"

Their mother nodded, "Good... a little salty, though."

Rayon felt what little hairs she had left stand up.

"Dad liked his soup cooked with flavor, Ma," Rayon said.

"I know," their mother replied. "I just think it's

a little bit too salty."

"And I find yours bland," Rayon said. "You don't see me saying that though."

"Okay," Vy interjected. "Today is supposed to be about Dad, not us."

"How?" their mother asked. "By drinking soup?"

"No," Rayon snapped. "By trying to hold on to him."

Her mother put her spoon down and intertwined her fingers, "What do you have to hold on to? Duppie?"

Vy said, "Mom, please…"

"It's okay, Vy," Rayon said. "I'm trying to hold onto a memory Ma, do you know what that is…?"

Rayon stopped. She felt herself lifting above the room, where she was floating and looking down at a conversation shift into an argument. She watched from the ceiling fan as so much inaudible anger took wind. As her mother threw blows about everything she couldn't stand about her— the apartment and soup and job and ex-girlfriend and newfangled baldness, and, for the first time, Rayon's response. Her mother's judgmental nature, closed-mindedness, bigotry, ignorance, and hella unsalted soup. Rayon was beginning to rage, and she watched herself morph into a person that was capable of it. The apartment looked different from that angle. She figured it would, but not that much. It seemed smaller, tighter, stuffy and cramped. Which was odd, because the thing Rayon loved most about it was the light it let in, and all the space she had. Rayon floated down into her body, red eyes and a sore throat.

"We don't even know what happened to him," Rayon said. "If he suffered or not. How can you not care? Wasn't there any love there?"

Her mother stood and gave her an under-eyed glance. She headed for the door and said, "There still is, and always will be."

Rayon's heart stopped, or skipped a beat, one of the two. Their eyes met and locked on each other like they were seeing the other for the first time. Greif was funny that way, Rayon understood — like swimming against the current in the hopes of finding, of finding. Their mother left in a near huff, and as Vy followed looking back, grinning a soft grin only her sister could see.

"I like this Rayon," Vy winked and walked down behind their mother.

As the words fell off of her sister's lips, Rayon realized that she liked her too. She went to the bathroom and looked at herself again. Hairless and perm free. She ran her hand across her scalp, feeling the pricks of hair embed themselves into her skin. She felt connected, without a type of band or rope pulling her further away from herself. Rayon looked at herself and smiled, the kind of smile that made the room and anyone in it light up. She left and picked up her phone before heading for the street. The thought of grabbing the subway not even crossing her mind, she would run or float the way she did before, she would fly to Brooklyn.

Her heart hummed on the way to Stacy's house, didn't feel like it was beating at all. She could hear the reggaeton though, popping through her pulse like the music was radiating from inside. With each stride the music became more prominent, her footsteps following a beat that only she could hear. She ran all the way to Stacy's studio, and she wasn't tired. She rang up and was buzzed in seconds later, like Stacy knew she was coming. Rayon entered Stacy's space and felt a whirlwind of senses. The plush rug beneath her soles, the smell of curry and recently exploded bath bombs. They'd been so happy here, Rayon hated that they'd been so heated as well.

"Why won't you stop calling me," Rayon abruptly asked.

Stacy took a step back, "Because I love you."

"But I don't think love is enough," Rayon whispered.

"Doesn't it have to be?"

Rayon stepped closer to Stacy and took her by the hand. She rubbed her finger tips over Stacy's knuckles and watched her lover quiver in the unknown.

Rayon shook her head and said, "No, Stac... There has to be more."

She touched Stacy's face and felt herself become just as vulnerable as her partner—it'd be easy to fall right back into her, but to learn to say no, not because of logic or reason, but because we just knew we needed to say it. That was completely new territory for Rayon. Territory she felt stronger in, perhaps, more like herself.

Rayon went back outside and prepared to take off running back home, but when she took her first step, her foot floated off the ground like it did in her apartment. She lifted up and looked down at the city she felt more apart of than before. When she took her job as a community organizer years earlier, she wasn't exactly sure why she did, it just felt right, but looking down at the city this way, it became so clear. The Bronx was settled north of the place she used to know, sitting on top of the burrow so many people focused on. That didn't make it any less a part of the city though. It was a place Rayon feared would soon be changed, altered to suit some other need. There was nothing wrong with it the way it was. Rayon landed on the roof of the triplex, unsure of how to get down. Instead, she sat on the ledge, barely smelling the red pea soup from her apartment, and knowing, not out of logic or reason, just knowing; that he didn't suffer, her father, not then anyway. Not in death. Not in a home where he so often tasted the splendor of salted red peas.

Sometimes Rayon would walk back to the block Cromartie Street used to be on and just sit, for hours at a time, she'd sit and dwell on the place she was sure she'd never see again. When the block was quiet and the rest of the street signs would light up in that same neon green, there were times she'd see one of those small purple flowers. Never on a patch of grass though, usually next to a sewage drain or beneath loose road rubble on the side of the street. She grabbed one once, it was rooted in the cement like it belonged to the burrow, unmoved or phased by the attempt to pull it from where it was. Rayon never actually tried to pry one out, the little purple flowers, instead she basked in their supreme beauty on the off chance she saw one, somewhere near where Cromartie Street used to be.

12 Steps

1. Powerless

Explain that it's bigger than you. That she can't possibly understand because she is young and inexperienced. Watch her roll her eyes because she is not so young anymore, because she is experienced, because you made her grow up too fast. Act like you don't see her roll her eyes, pretend you don't know why she rolled them. Tell her that her behavior is unbecoming. Tense up when she yells the same thing at you. Get up in a fury because she raised her voice, ask her who the hell she thinks she is. Feel your heart skip a beat when she says, "my father's daughter" and rolls her eyes again. Bite your lip before you say the thing you immediately wish you didn't say. Feel the words creeping up your throat and tickling your tongue. Mumble under your breath, "and you wonder why I drink..." See her staring at you, fully aware that she heard her father blame his daughter for a problem he's had since before she was born. Watch her stand up and wonder when she got so tall, notice that she has put on weight, as well. Watch her grab your Heineken and launch it at the fridge before you can react. Wince at the sound of the bottle shattering into what sounds like a thousand pieces, look down at those pieces before you look back at her. Realize what a good arm she has. Think about reaching across the table, not to hurt her, just to scare her. Don't. Stand there motionless as she storms off and you hear the front door slam behind her. Worry that she might not come home this time as you tiptoe over the broken glass and grab another beer from the fridge. Open the bottle and sit back down to finish your meal. Pause a second and try to remember how the argument started as you sip your Heineken.

2. Greater Than

Stay up downing a mixture of rum and whiskey until 3:04A.M., convince yourself you are doing it because she has not come home. Pretend that this is not your nightly routine. Leave another message for her, "Jemma, you better not be at that little dick's place. Come home, now!" Hear how sober you sound before hanging up as you shut your eyes so the spinning stops. Think about that article she brought you three years ago, the one about functioning alcoholics. Remember glancing at her under-eyed and tossing it on the coffee table before gnarling, "Where does an eighth grader find shit like this." Remember her response, "I'm in grade nine." Remember waiting until she went into the kitchen to pick up the article, remember reading about susceptibility levels increasing with time, remember the same paragraph stressing the fact that that doesn't mean you have it under control. Remember reaching for the last bottle of your four pack, remember reading that there is always something more to live for than an addiction. Remember peeking in the kitchen and seeing her make a PB&J, watching her spread the peanut butter as methodically as she'd brush her teeth, iron her clothes, and count her babysitting money. Money you asked her to borrow the day after she worked, money you still need to give back to her. Remember smiling as she put the sandwich together and called out, "Do you want a snack, Dad?" and you saying, "No." Remember the weight of the bottle in your left hand against that of the article in the right, how much heavier it was. Remember hearing her coming back towards the den, remember tossing the article away before she came through. Remember staring at her hair and thinking about how much it looked like her mother's. Remember gulping a mouthful of Budweiser as the article brushed the bottom of your heal. Call Jemma, again.

3. *Decide*

Pass out then wake up an hour later. Stand up and stagger to her room, see that she still isn't home. Grab your car keys and get in the pickup. Back out of the driveway and clip the trash can, remember to put the trash out tomorrow. Take off faster than you should because you are angry, angry that she hasn't come home, but mostly, because you know where she is. Swerve a bit because your eyes are still adjusting, get angrier because you have to be at work in a few hours and instead of sleeping you're out swerving in the street to pick up your seventeen-year-old from her twenty-year-old boyfriend's house. Get even angrier because the thought of it all pisses you off so much. Get to his house nine minutes later and bang on the front door as loud as you can. Wait too long before he opens the door and says, "Hey, Anok... Sup?" Answer him, "It's Mr. Sellers... Tell Jemma to get out here." Watch his left eyebrow raise and that roguish smirk creep across his face, "She's getting dressed." Feel yourself become tense and your right hand turn to a fist. Close your eyes and take a deep breath. You want to punch him hard in the face but remind yourself that this kid could kick your ass, that he is five inches taller and eight inches broader; that you already have two strikes and a third would mean you go away and she would end up living here, with him. Open your eyes. See that Jemma is standing in front of you with her arms crossed. Motion to the car and start walking towards it, feel her grab the keys from your pocket. Think about demanding them back, but know she knows you well enough to tell when you've been drinking. Know she knows that's almost all the time. Get in the passenger seat before she pulls out real smooth, take notice of what a good driver she is. Remember that you didn't teach her, because she refused to let you. Say, "I could have him arrested, you know… You're seventeen!" Listen to her not respond. Feel the quiet between the two of you. Look at her and see the tear forming that she'll refuse to let fall. Listen to her whisper, "You have to decide, Dad…" Pretend to have no idea what's she's talking about.

4. Fearless

Remember knocking out in the truck as you wake up to the obnoxious beep of your alarm, wonder how you got there. Figure Jemma helped you in-side after the hours of binging had finally caught up. Have the passing thought that she has tucked you in just as much as you have tucked her. Get up and be overcome by nausea, stand still for a moment as it passes. Go to the kitchen and get the coffee started. Get in a cold shower. Feel the heavy streams whip your face as the nausea comes back, lean forward and feel the water beating your bald spot. Feel it coming up. Wretch, loudly. Vom-it smooth streams of yellow and watch it splash around your toes before going down the drain. Continue to vomit until your stomach is empty then get out of the shower. Start brushing your teeth and see the remnants of smooth yellow in the corners of your mouth as you watch yourself in the mirror. Stop brushing, wipe the yellow away, but keep staring. Think about what Jemma said in the truck, realize just how much it scared you. Remember when her mother told you to make the same decision, remember your choice. Remember thinking to yourself, *trying and failing would mean you weren't strong enough*. Question your strength as you examine the bags and crow's feet around your eyes, then think about how strong your daughter must be to drag her incapacitated father into bed. Look at yourself again and say under your breath, "I can do this."

5. Admit

Come home early on the fifth afternoon of your sobriety with two six packs and immediately regret throwing all of the rest of your liquor away. Remember why you did it; telling Jemma you were giving it up, remember her sarcastic, "Okay". Remember asking her to help you get rid of it all five days ago, so she would take you seriously, remember the passing glance she threw you after the two of you wiped the house clean and dumped every stash out. Remember the way her eyes glittered and the almost smile she gave you, remember the warmth you felt. Remember trying to recall the last time she looked at you that way. Remember that look, it's the only thing that's gotten you through the past week. The shaky week, so much so that there were times you couldn't steady your hands enough to work the line. So much so that your co-workers noticed and asked you if you were feeling alright. The week of migraines and not being able to remember much of anything, the week of your heart beating so fast you thought it might explode. So much so that you thought about going to the doctor, but instead left work early and picked up two six packs on the way home. Take the six packs into your room and promise yourself you're just having one, just so you don't kill yourself trying to do this thing cold turkey. Finish a can in less than three minutes, lick your lips as the after taste of cool bitterness resonates on your tongue. Look at the six packs and start reaching for one more, try to stop yourself by remembering that look, grab one anyway. Just one, more. Start drinking. Be startled when you hear her come in the house. Scurry around your room looking for a good hiding spot for the beers, settle on the top of your closet behind the winter sweaters. Hurry back to your bed and pretend to be napping when she knocks. Say, "Come in." Hear the door creek but keep your back to her as she asks, "What are you doing home so early?" Say, "Wasn't feeling well, thought I'd come rest a bit." Listen to the quiet, be tempted to turn around to see what she's doing. Don't. Wonder if she can smell the beer on your breath even though you're not facing her, wonder if she spotted the open closet door you didn't have time to shut. Listen to her as she asks, "Dad, have you been keeping clean?" Lie, "Of course, I said I would, didn't I?" Listen to her walk out without answering, but because you know her, know she nodded. Jump up and lock your door quietly, go back to the closet and get your booze, down every last can in an hour. Before knocking out, realize the real reason you didn't look at her was because you were worried she'd have that look on her face, again. Worried that it might have been enough to keep you from finishing what was behind the sweaters.

6. Defects

Become meticulous at hiding your stashes. Keep them in the places she hates going, your bedroom, the garage, and her mother's old work-space, even though you converted it into a spare bedroom thirteen years ago when she left. Hide whiskey bottles in your tool-boxes, beer cans in your work boots, and rum in your dirty laundry. Only down them after she's turned in, and don't be bothered by only having warm ones to drink. Hide your bottles behind you one night when you hear her get out of bed and walk towards the living room. Pretend to be engrossed in the game. Feel her flop down beside you and stiffen your back so the bottles don't rattle. Say, "What are you doing up?" Listen to her respond, "I'm not tired..." Wait for her to go on, you can tell she has something else to say, "I'm really proud of you. It'll be two weeks, tomorrow." Don't answer, just nod and keep your eyes on the television. She goes on to tell you to make sure to be home by six o'clock tomorrow, she's decided to make dinner to celebrate your accomplishment. Feel yourself tense as she takes hold of your chin, turns your face towards hers then says, "I love you, Dad." Smile at her before saying, "I love you, too." Feel her arms wrap around your neck and let the tension melt away, stuff your face deep into the crevasse between her shoulder and neck and wrap your arms around her back. Hold her tightly, the way you did the night you had to tell her that her mother wasn't coming back; the night you drank yourself into the stupor you stayed in for a week. Feel her arms loosening from around your neck and let her go. Look at her. Notice that her face looks rounder than usual, realize you're probably only noticing this because the two of you haven't been this close in a long time. Feel strange moisture on the nape of your back. Nearly jump up but then remember the half empty bottle you were hiding and figure it tipped over when you hugged her. Lean back, quickly. Say, "Alright, you have until the end of the quarter." Put your arm around her and feel her snuggle up, remember how this feels. Send her to bed in five minutes, then dispose of the empty bottles behind you. Get an old rag and scrub the couch clean. Go to your room to change your beer stained clothing before going to bed.

7. Humility

Get off work and head straight home, no, stop at the bakery at the corner first. If she is making dinner, the least you could do is get dessert. Ask the lady behind the counter if they have any Boston cream pie, Jemma's favorite, listen to the lady say, "No, but we will in the morning." Blow, loudly. Buy an assortment of fruit tarts instead, her second favorite, and get home five minute before six. Be surprised by how good the house smells, beef stroganoff, wonder when she learned to cook such a thing. Realize this is the first time you've smelt the dish in over a decade, realize you haven't eaten it since her mother left. Take the fruit tarts into the kitchen and tell her everything smells great. Notice that she doesn't make eye contact with you when she responds, "Thanks." Wash your hands then sit down at the already set table. Lick your lips as she portions the stroganoff into both of your plates. Pick up your fork, stop, she's staring at you. Say, "What?" Watch her face soften before responding, "This is a real milestone, you know. Two weeks!" Nod and glance down at your plate before she goes on, "I didn't think you'd be able to do it without help, but here we are." Nod again, but this time say, "I told you..." Watch her nod before she says, "You did. Oh, I forgot the drinks." Take in a big mouthful of stroganoff, salivate a little, be consumed by the decadent flavor and rich aromas. Listen to Jemma open the fridge and say, "What'll it be, dad?" Shoot your eyes in her direction and watch her pull your hidden liquor out of the fridge—your tool box whiskey, dirty linen rum, and work boot beer cans. Watch her turn around, cross her arms, and stare at you with your mouth full of stroganoff. Almost choke when she raises her voice, "WELL?" Chew profusely as she brings you a beer and pops the can open, swallow. Say, "I can explain." Listen to her say, "You don't have to." Be stumped. Don't say a word. Watch her eat the meal she prepared for the two of you to celebrate your sobriety, still don't say anything. Take another bite of stroganoff then sip the beer she opened for you.

8. The List

Wake up the following morning and see that a lot of her stuff is gone: toothbrush, bathrobe, jacket, shoes, backpack, and small suitcase, be relieved she didn't take the big one. Go into the kitchen to call her with your apology, see a note on the kitchen table. Read it:

Dad, I understand that this is a process, but I think that in order for you to do this, something needs to be a stake… I'm staying with Mike until you A) Dispose of ALL the alcohol hidden in the house, B) Readmit yourself into AA, C) MAKE YOUR SOBRIETY THE PRIORITY – not me, not work, SOBRIETY D) Get and stay clean for *at least <u>two weeks</u>. Once you do everything on this list, we'll talk. I'm not competing anymore, dad, I shouldn't have to... you shouldn't want me to. ~Jem*

Feel your eyes welting up, don't cry. Be tempted to call Jemma, don't. Realize that she had every right to do what she did, except for giving you another chance, you don't deserve one. Go to the cabinet and grab a glass, then to the fridge and grab your rum. Sit down and pour yourself some. Stare at the burnt brown idling in front of you, don't cry. Push the glass off the table, and feel the rum splatter on your cheek. Bury your face in your palms and sink down into the chair. This time, cry. Cry loud and hard sobs as the tears in your hand form a shallow pool on your fingers. Feel your throat closing up as you gasp for air, realize you are hyperventilating. Push away from the table and put your head between your knees, panic, realize this has never happened before. Take long deep breaths, you heard this somewhere, realize it's not working. Stand up and grab your chest, it is starting to pinch. Find a brown bag to breathe into, you heard this somewhere, as well. Take five slow breaths into the bag. Feel your breathing even out. Realize you had an anxiety attack as you lean against the counter. Realize you are alone and had it been something more, it would have been days before someone found you. Cover your mouth and close your eyes, think about that look, think about feeling her in your arms. Open your eyes. Take out your cell phone to call the AA group you were assigned to after the first two D.U.Is, realize you deleted the number. Hurry to your room and start digging through your night stand. Dig and dig and dig and dig until you find the card of the group's organizer. Dial and wait for her to pick up. Explain that you want to rejoin, listen to her not respond. Wait. Listen as she finally asks you, "Mr. Sellers, not to seem discouraging, but you've been in our program twice already, and once your probation was over, you quit. What makes this time any different?" Pause, think about that look again, say, "I think this is my last chance."

9. Amends

Mark '14' on the calendar. Clean out the house the following day. Look through spots you're sure you haven't hidden a stash, just in case. Be tempted to go on a final binge before throwing everything out, just taste a sip of the Russian whiskey a buddy gave you instead. Wonder if that buddy knows you drink...drank, figure everyone knew. Drink a quarter of the bottle, then throw it away. Brush your teeth, you need to get the smell of whiskey off your breath before AA. Go to the meeting. Sign in. Sigh in relief when you see it is not a circle set up, sit at the back of the room. Don't socialize, not even with the woman you recognize from your past experiences in the group. Pretend not to notice her staring at you with those clear brown eyes you can see sparkling from across the room, fiddle with your phone until the meeting starts, instead. Listen as the groups organizer says, "We have a few more people joining us, tonight. If it's your first time, or first time back in a while, come on up the front— tell us why you are here." Want to stay seated, but realize that would only draw more attention. Be the last person to get to the front and wait for the two men in front of you to speak. Ignore them as you try to figure out what to say. Think hard, so hard you realize you are making a face. Stop. Watch the man in front of you return to his seat. Keep your hands deep down in your pockets as you feel the room on your shoulders, every eye, every breath, everything. Say, "Hi, I'm Anok," Pause. Fidget a little before going on, "and I'm one of the 'first time back in a while' folks." Listen to the room chuckle a bit, take a breath. Go on, "I'd like to say I'm here because I choose to be, and that's sort of true, but mostly…" Look out onto the room of people before finishing your thought, "I owe it to someone."

10. Admit It

Mark '11' on the calendar. Go to a walk-in clinic instead of work three days after the first AA meeting because the shakiness and other crap have come back. Find out they are not uncommon symptoms of withdrawal. Listen to the inpatient recommendation given by the doctor after you mention living alone, lie, "I'll think about it." Pocket your prescriptions, Chlordiazepoxide and Propranolol, listen to the doctor say, "They should be ready first thing tomorrow morning." Shake the doctor's hand and check the time. Decide to go see Jemma before heading to AA, you want to show her your prescriptions. See her sitting on the patio when you drive up. Smile and wave as you walk towards her, watch her glance away. Listen to her say, "We're nowhere near two weeks, you know." Shake your head in agreement, "I know, I just want to show you these," dig the prescriptions out of your pocket and hand them to her, "They're supposed to help me with the symptoms." Look at her examine them, "You actually went to the doctor?" Grin and sit down beside her, "Clinic." Realize that was the first time you had seen a doctor in over a decade. Say, "I'm back in AA, too." Watch her nod as she stares at your prescriptions. Sit in silence for a while then be surprised when she asks, "Did mom regret having me?" Frown your face up before replying, "Why would you ask that?" Listen to her response, "She left..." Say, "Me!" Listen to her say, "Us... Did she regret it?" Pause before saying, "I didn't." Watch her burst into a wail of laughter before saying, "Says the alcoholic!" Don't smile, just say, "Says your dad..." Listen to her repeat, "The alcoholic!" Listen to her laughter die down and realize just how strange the question was, want to ask more about it, but understand she'll only deflect again. She is her father's daughter, remember. Stand up and say, "I should get going, AA starts soon." Take the prescriptions back as she stands up. Want to hug her, don't. Want to tell her that all of this is scaring the shit out of you, don't; that you wish she was home, that you miss her, that you love her. Don't. Just say, "Guess I'll see you later," then turn around and walk to your truck. Hear her call out, "Dad!" Look back at her. Listen to her say, "Eleven days." Smile when you realize she is counting down, too. Nod. Get in the truck and go to AA. Be approached by the sparkly eyed woman you remembered as you sign in. Hear her say, "Remember me?" Lie, "Sort of." Watch her extend her hand, "I'm Sheila. Nice to meet you, Anok." Tense up as you shake her hand and say, "Hey, I'm Anok." Remember that she just called you by name. Look away so she doesn't see you flushed. Walk into the room together and listen to her say, "I've noticed that every time you come back you avoid mentioning the real reason you're here. The reason we're all here." Look at her and say, "What do you mean?" Watch her shrug before sitting down beside her. Repeat yourself, "What are you talking about?" Listen to her shush you before the meeting starts. Think about what she said as a new woman introduces herself and goes on to say, "I'm an alcoholic, and I've been fighting this thing way too long... I need help." Feel Sheila's head turn and glance down at her. Notice how attractive she is before realizing why she looked at you. Look away. Wait until after the meeting to say what you have to say to her, "I might not talk about it, Sheila, but my being here makes damn sure that it's known." Watch her eyes widen before you feel content enough in your zinger to leave, then feel her grab your arm. Watch her take out a pen and write a phone number on your palm. Feel her caress your arm before she leaves you sitting there. Contemplate. Call that number half an hour after you get home. Talk to Sheila about more than you expected to for the rest of the night.

11. Consciousness

Continue to count down the days and don't take a single drink. Go out for coffee with Sheila twice

and invite her out to dinner next week. Continue
with AA and vomit more than a few times. Call
Jemma every other day, tell her you can't wait for
her to come home. Take up an old hobby; reading. Go to a used bookstore and buy a bag of dollar novels, lie to the cashier when she comments
on how many you have, say they are to pass the
time. Think about the real reason being you need
a distraction; something to keep your hands and
mind busy. Read all the time; at home, on break,
at lunch, before bed, all the time. Realize you're
also using reading as a way to withdraw because
you sense yourself getting snippy. So much so
that you told your manager to screw off a few
days ago and the only reason he didn't write you
up being that you were a twenty year worker, that
it was the first time he'd ever had a problem with
you, that it was obvious you are going through
something and that he wanted you to get through
it. Remember shaking his hand and apologiz-
ing, "It won't happen again." Say, "No thanks,"
to the guys at work when they invite you out for
a beer. Go home and keep reading. Read as the
days pass, Robertson and Poe and Austen and
Mosley and James and Reid. Read and remember how much you enjoy it. Go to bed the night
before you will pick up Jemma and think about
how much she looks like your ex-wife. Wonder

what she did with her life. Wonder how she can live that life knowing she abandoned her daughter. Stop thinking about it because it's making you crave a shot. Pause. Realize what you just did and force yourself to keep wondering. Wonder if she'll ever call Jemma, or if she already has and it's a secret they're keeping from you. Wonder if she had more children, if Jemma is a big a sister. Wonder what type of man she ended up with, or if she started dating women. Pause and cover yourself in the sheets. Wonder how terrible things must have been for her to leave you both, not just the man that drank, cheated, and slapped her; but the daughter that would undoubtedly remind her of that man every day. Wonder and then sleep. Wake up the next morning and write '0' on the calendar. Get ready to go get Jemma but notice that her door is cracked. Peek inside her room and see that she is there, she is here, see that she came home on her own.

12. Pass On

Stay clean for another month. Keep going to AA and introduce Sheila to Jemma. Make dinner for the three of you, beef stroganoff, and listen to Jemma tell Sheila about her breakup with the little dick, "I mean, we started dating in high school and are in completely different places now..."

Listen to Sheila's compassion and understanding even though you know she knows what actual hardship is. Feel something you haven't felt in a long time when Sheila kisses you goodnight. Want to ask her to stay over, don't, for Jemma's sake. Rejoin Jemma in the kitchen and notice that her weight is back down, that her face is no longer round. Think about asking her about it, don't. Think again, don't. Understand that she'll talk to you about it one day, if she chooses to. Catch yourself staring at her, keep staring when she looks at you. Listen to her ask, "What?" Say, "You make me really happy…" Laugh when she says, "Happier than, Sheila?" Nod. Keep laughing when she says, "Happier than Heineken?" Say, "Happier than Heineken." Watch her smile, actually smile at you. Watch the corners of her mouth curve upward towards her full almond eyes and her cheeks lift into high dollops of what you imagine is pure serenity. Swear that this won't be the last time she smiles at you for what would feel like ages. Listen to her as she asks, "What was different this time, Dad?" Say, "It isn't over, never will be, Jemma…" Listen to her say, "I know, but what was it?" Stare at her, hard. Explore the eyes you suddenly realize are a dead ringer for your own, just bigger, fuller. Look at them and realize she already knows the answer. Promise to never let her forget it.

The Coyote

"I'm going to kill him," Maria shouted as she came in the house.

"What happened this time?" Kiren asked.

Maria flopped down on the sofa, "The same thing that happens every day; Doucherson makes it a point to shit on me in front of the entire staff. You know he told me to go wipe down the staff bathroom today because housekeeping had to cancel… me! I mean, what the hell do I look like?"

Maria immediately realized her tirade might have come off as offensive to Kiren, especially considering his mother cleaned houses for forty years.

"Not that there's anything wrong with that," Maria went on. "But I'm the assistant manager you know, it's so damn disrespectful."

"I know, babe. It'll get better…"

"It's been four months, Kiren, when?" Maria said. "What the hell did I do to this guy? I want to go home."

"This is home now, Maria. You knew the company was relocating when you made me buy you that," Kiren said as he motioned to her finger.

Maria fiddled with her engagement ring, "I know."

"As for your boss," Kiren stood. "This is Vegas, play your cards right and things will work out."

She nodded before asking, still fiddling with her ring. "You wanted it too, Kiren. You just needed a push."

Kiren grinned the wide mouthed grin Maria melted over ever since they met three years earlier. It hadn't felt nearly that long. Kiren twisted his fingers between Maria's and traced her knuckles like they were a thing of beauty. They made love that night. Maria couldn't get to sleep afterwards, and it was because of Eric Wilkerson, better known as Doucherson. The disdain she felt for that man exceeded any measure of loathing Maria knew herself capable of.

It wasn't the reality of a less-qualified manager spouting off orders that irked her, but that he made a point of rubbing his authority in everyone's face; that was the kicker. Doucherson didn't hire Maria; she was sent to the retail powerhouse directly from upper management, better known as Kiren's company's brand-manager's brother-in-law. Maria was sure Doucherson would fire her if he could, but affirmative action terrified him. So instead, he turned every day into a head-piercing migraine — the snide commentary, constant second guessing, micromanagement, or overall jerkish attitude. She just couldn't stand him.

Maria went into the kitchen for a cup of Chamomile tea, she needed something to help put her to sleep. As she waited for the water to boil, she heard a commotion coming from outside. All the windows were shut, so she figured the volume alone was worth checking out. She walked into the living room, peeked out the blinds and saw a cluster of cats fleeing from the dumpster. When the dust had cleared, there were only two animals left, a wide-eyed cat and what looked like a soft brown coyote. She examined it closely underneath the trembling street light, it's pointed ears, thin frame and long nose, then she was sure.

Maria thought of the first time she saw a coyote. She was driving home, close to midnight, after having a last-minute task dropped on her lap by Doucherson; she saw something skirt across the road. She remembered thinking it resembled a strange-looking dog, that its face was thin and wide, like Wile E. Then it hit her, just as the brick wall would smack Wile E as fiercely as it always did — a coyote.

Maria watched the coyote, long and slender, approach the lone cat. Its strides were smooth and strong, and its back blades rolled more like a wild cat than a canine. Each step was so precise; it was as if the coyote didn't realize the cat was staring directly at it. Unlike the others, this cat stood its ground, its tail fluffed towards the dumpster and paw pointed at the slowly approaching beast. Maria watched the cat's mouth spread and teeth begin to show. The closer the coyote got, the more the cat's back would bend, and the bigger its tail expanded. The coyote was only inches away now, and the cat still hadn't budged.

The kettle whistled and Maria nearly jumped out of her skin. She darted to the kitchen and removed it from the burner before returning to the window. When she got back, both the coyote and the cat were gone. Maria walked to the door and stepped outside.

"Where'd they go?" she mumbled quietly.

It was as if nothing had happened, the street was quiet and the night empty. No cat and no coyote.

The next morning, she told Kiren about what she saw.

He glanced at her over his coffee, "You sure you weren't dreaming?"

"Kiren," Maria huffed. "Of course, I'm sure. I think it was a si—"

Kiren's phone rang. He gestured for her to hold on and answered. There was some emergency at work, Maria already figured, there always was when he got early morning calls.

Kiren mouthed, "Got to go."

He kissed her forward as she whispered, "Don't forget we're meeting the florist today."

Kiren left in a hurry, without a word, and Maria arrived at work an hour later. Doucherson wasn't getting in until noon, and Maria relished in the peace that was a slow morning. At about one o'clock everyone had taken their lunch breaks and Maria was heading towards the staff room to take hers, until she was stopped by Doucherson near the register.

"Excuse me," he said. "Where are you going?"

"To lunch," she replied.

Doucherson puffed up his chest, "You should be confirming that with me on a daily basis, we don't eat until staff has."

"I make the lunch schedule," Maria sighed. "I know when everyone has eaten."

"Do you?"

Maria felt herself becoming tense, "Yes."

"Well, depending on foot traffic we both need to be out here. So, take lunch at two."

Maria looked around the empty store and felt herself chomping down on her own tongue. She was about to swallow her words, but then she thought of the cat. It's arched back, sparkling teeth, and the hissing sound she couldn't hear. She thought of it as she balled her fist so tightly her nails pierced her palm, and the hairs on her neck stood with a vengeance. Maria thought about pounding the counter, hitting it so hard Doucherson would jump, but she didn't.

She released her fist and calmly said, "Fuck off."

Doucherson's face became flush red, "What did you s—"

"I wasn't sure what it was… I almost started trying to convince myself that it was me, something I did," Maria stepped closer to him, her strides strong and smooth. "But it's not, it's just you."

Doucherson didn't speak.

Maria continued, "Where do you get off talking to me like that? Where do you get off talking to anyone like that? I don't like you, Erik, and you don't like me. We don't have to like each other, but just a shred of decency can go pretty damn far. You're arrogance and ill-mannered nature turn my stomach as much as the shit you seem to get off on having me clean."

"Well someone has to do it—"

"Have you?" Maria replied sharply as her tone elevated. "Have you? You're lucky you still have this job, I should be running this—"

An inaudible sound began coming from his mouth, like a dying bird gasping for air. Maria looked at his face closely and noticed that it wasn't red from anger, but that the man was crying. Wide eyed and frozen, he sobbed big dewy tears. He cried like a child, wheezily, and he wouldn't stop. Maria pulled him around the corner as he began to hyperventilate.

"Breathe, Erik," Maria coached. "Take deep breaths."

"I didn't know what else to do," Doucherson stuttered. "Management calls me up and tells me they're sending someone over and here you come. More experience, better references... You're my fucking replacement."

Maria shook her head, "That's not true."

"Yes it is," he wiped his wet face. "I have a family, Maria. Two kids and another one on the way; I can't lose this job."

"But that doesn't give you the right to treat people like thi—"

"I know," he interrupted. "But what else am I

supposed to do?"

Maria watched him quiver and felt herself soften. It wasn't that she felt sorry for Doucherson; she just understood him. She told him she'd close up; to go home.

Maria called Kiren a minute later.

"Hey, babe," Kiren answered.

"Hey, we have to reschedule our appointment with the florist."

"Fine," Kiren quickly replied. "You never finished this morning, what sort of sign was the dream?"

Maria wanted to repeat that it wasn't a dream, but said, "That I was supposed to stand up for myself; like the cat did to the coyote."

Kiren responded, quickly again, "You sure you're the cat?"

Maria heard a tone in his voice that caught her off guard.

She asked, "When should I reschedule our meeting with the florist?"

Kiren was silent, it was as if she hadn't asked the question. The other line was as quiet as the night before, after the cat and coyote disappeared, into the emptiness.

Dry Dreams

Sumaya awoke out of breath. The sensation was so intense she knew it was real. Her legs were still numb and the remnant of that distinct throb still present. She reached for the seat of her underwear and rubbed her thumb against the dry lace. She exhaled a long, solemn sigh. Raj touched her shoulder and she jumped a bit.

"What's wrong?" he asked.

"Nothing," she replied. "It's just... I think it happened again."

Raj sat up and glanced at her hand hidden within the lingerie he bought her the week before.

He asked, "Are you sure?"

She nodded.

"What was the dream about?"

Sumaya considered lying to him. She considered lying because she knew what Raj really wanted to know; because the answer was no, it always had been. Sumaya heard what Raj really asked as clear as the moon outside their one bay window; it was all they could afford at the time when Sumaya insisted on some renovations to make their studio appear larger. It was small and unassuming, the window, and much too expensive.

"We could have had six regular windows put in at this price…" Raj said.

"I like bay windows more," she replied. "Don't you?"

They installed the one bay window and Sumaya sat her favorite chair next to it. She'd read in the chair, watch TV, and sometimes just look out onto the barren side street. She did it because she loved that bay window and she wanted Raj to remember that.

"You don't have to tell me," Raj whispered. "Only if you want to."

Sumaya turned and got out of bed. She closed the bathroom door behind her as Raj slumped back down into the sheets. He regretted asking her the question, it was the one thing Dr. Jenks told him not to do.

"People's dreams are their own, Rajit," Dr. Jenks said. "Sumaya needs to be able to explore hers freely, and not feel guilty or obligated to share them."

He wanted to protest, to say he only asked because he cared, but he said nothing. He nodded and listened to Sumaya ask Dr. Jenks a slew of questions for the remainder of their session.

They started the sessions a year and half after they started dating. Raj travelled a lot for work, and Sumaya suggested they speak with someone about ways to keep their connection intact. Raj went along, reluctantly. *It was unheard of,* Raj's mother had said when she found out about the sessions. *That sort of therapy, and before marriage... unheard of.*

Sumaya locked the bathroom door — she knew she didn't need to, Raj would never walk in without knocking, but the impulse was to lock it before she got in the tub. She pulled the shower head off and placed the removable head between her thighs, adjusting the water pressure to the highest setting. Sumaya stood and thought about the first time she experienced a sleep orgasm. The dream was so vivid, she pleasured herself into a fury, and when she reached climax, she woke in pure confusion.

She sat up, quickly, letting out a loud gasp as

she did.

"You okay?" Raj mumbled.

"I don't know," Sumaya said, balling her fist and pressing it to her beating heart.

"What's the matter?" Raj asked, still not fully awake.

"I came," Sumaya said.

"What?" Raj replied.

"I just had an orgasm," she said. "Well, I think."

"In your sleep? Like a wet dream?" he asked.

"Yeah," Sumaya checked herself. "I'm not wet, though. Completely dry."

"So how do you know you had one?"

"I just know," she said.

Sumaya did some research the following day and looked up information on human anatomy, focusing on reproductive and sexual organs. She looked for the term 'sleep orgasm' first, then specified, 'female sleep orgasm.' She found a few articles, made copies, and took them home to show Raj. He glanced at the articles before bed that night and the two read in silence.

Sumaya said, "See, it's a real thing…"

Raj shrugged, "Guess so."

He got under the covers and closed his eyes.

"What!" Sumaya said. "Are you mad or something?"

"I'm just tired, Sumaya. Going to sleep."

She paused before she asked, "Do we need to talk about this?"

"No," Raj answered.

"I think we need to talk about this," Sumaya said.

Raj didn't answer.

"Raj," Sumaya said. "Raj?"

He was pretending to be asleep, Sumaya knew it, and Raj knew she knew it, but he continued pretending, and she continued pretending she didn't know he was pretending.

Raj heard the water running in the bathroom and wondered if Sumaya took hot or cold showers. They'd been living together for two years, and he never thought to ask her. He once considered joining her, surprising her in the shower and hopping in, but when he went to open the door, it was locked. He also never thought to ask Sumaya to be his wife. Their three-year relationship might have warranted it, but he never thought to ask. He knew that if Sumaya wanted him to, he'd know it. Just like he knew about the bay window, locked bathroom door, and her sleep orgasms. He'd know.

Sumaya turned the water off and wrapped herself in a towel. She stood in front of the mirror and wiped the condensation away. She began to lather her cheeks — her pores were clogged — a routine she'd taken to since before she and Raj moved in together. He asked her if she would move in with him on their one-year anniversary. He rented out a local bakery — the laddu was to die for, and he brought in a firestorm of candles, roses, and other romantic tidbits. He was shy about it, asking her at first; she thought he was preparing for a proposal, but that seemed a bit sudden, a bit rushed. He went on to ask her to move in after she hinted at the necessity of two people living together before marriage nowadays, *it wasn't the Stone Age.*

Sumaya splashed her face and went back into the bedroom. Raj was sitting up.

"Are you okay?"

"Yeah," she replied.

Raj paused before he asked, "Are you sure?"

"Of course," Sumaya said.

Sumaya got back into bed and Raj crossed his arms, staring at the window.

He said, "It doesn't make sense; having one window."

"Why do you always come back to the window?" Sumaya asked. "It's like you're obsessed with it or something."

"I'm not," Raj said. "I just think we should have gotten more of the regular ones."

"And you're always so concerned about money," Sumaya faced Raj. "I know the others were cheaper but I li—"

"It's not about the money, Sumi," Raj interrupted. "It's because they'd let more light in."

Sumaya was still. She stared at Raj as he sat naked under the covers, still staring at the window.

Raj asked, "Why do you lock the door when you use the bathroom?"

Sumaya hesitated, "I don't know. Never really thought about it."

Raj looked at her then, "Yes you have. Why?"

Sumaya shrugged, "Well, you're gone so much, and I read somewhere that it isn't good to leave yourself vulnerable, especially at home. And showers are some of the most vulnerable places you know... Break-ins and everything."

"You don't have to lock the door when I'm here, Sumaya."

"I know," she replied.

Raj leaned over and pressed his lips to Sumaya's neck, he kissed her softly then placed his hand on her inner thigh.

"What do you need me to do?" Raj asked.

"What?"

"To make you feel the way your dreams do."

Sumaya said, "Raj, Dr. Jenks said th—"

"I don't care about what she said," Raj interrupted, again. "I need to know what you want."

"I regret bringing it up at all," Sumaya said.

"Never regret telling the truth," Raj went on. "The only regret I have happened because I didn't listen to someone that I should have listened to. I don't want that to happen here."

"What was it?"

"What was what?"

"Your one regret?" Sumaya asked.

Raj slid his hand up her thigh as he said, "It doesn't matter."

Sumaya felt the pressure of Raj's fingers inside her. He pressed against everything and it made her feel contented and uncomfortable at the same time. Sumaya kissed him and he rolled on top of her. Raj felt around until he found it, the spot he'd never touched before, and Sumaya shuttered as she pulled him in closer.

Raj whispered, "I love you."

Sumaya grabbed hold of his wrist and pushed it further in. Raj dug down as Sumaya reacted a way neither were accustomed to, so he pressed his fingers deeper in.

"I love you, too," Sumaya whispered back.

Raj's fingers were starting to cramp as he realized he'd have to push harder than he wanted to for her to feel him, but he did. He nuzzled his head into her neck and felt her legs open slightly as her breathing became uneven. Raj fought his fingers from curling, he didn't care how long it took—Sumaya was finally coming.

THE STRANGER

I want there to be a mysterious stranger at my funeral. Standing in the back wearing a black fedora with a red feather and a brown trench coat. Brown because he will stand out amongst the sea of black, and red because it will suggest lust, passion, or love. I want him to be tall, over 6'2", that way he'll be taller than my husband, brother, and Doug. He would arrive late and wouldn't hold the door as it closed, he'd let it slam. Then he would stand beside the back pillar as all the seats would be taken, and even though everyone would be staring, he'd be looking straight ahead, at my casket. I want him to be one of the last to view my body. He would touch my hand, gently, and then he would look at my daughter. He would look at her but only for a second, just long enough for her to notice, and no one else. She would remember his face; his high cheekbones and strong jaw, smooth skin and tempered eyes.

I want her to look for him at the reception, but discover that he has gone and that no one saw him leave. Then she would find her Uncle and ask if he saw the man in brown with the black fedora and red feather. My brother would look at her over his plate of pie pieces and tarts, and he would lie, "Nope." She would leave and he would start scarfing down the sweets. He would gobble them up in less than five minutes and when the plate was empty, he would see his reflection in it. They'd be using the silver. He would stare at the cream in the corners of his mouth and then he would remember that time when he was seven. When he took the last two cupcakes that our mother was saving for our father, when he lied and said that he saw me eating them after he snuck the crummy plate into my bedroom. He would remember the beating I took that day, not because of the cupcakes, but because our mother said I lied about it. He would remember the day he became a liar. A skillful liar that would go on to pretend to have graduated from college, marry a sweet young woman, cheat on that woman two weeks after their marriage, father a son by the young escort he'd been sleeping with, leave his wife of seven years and their infant daughter for that escort, try to start a new life with the escort and son that would also end in divorce because he cheated on her too, call his second wife most every day after she left and tell her she was a dumb bitch, not be able to deny his adulterous ways in court because the escort wasn't such a dumb bitch after all, gain forty pounds and have to move in with his estranged sister. A liar that would cringe at the sight of his reflection because it reminded him of how much he loved sweets, and that he didn't know how to get his cravings under control.

I want her to look for Abagail and Doug next. She would find them sitting on the love seat with the torn, under-bottom as I would not have had the chance to have it reupholstered before my death. She would ask them if they saw the man in the brown jacket and black fedora with a red feather. Abagail would say, "Yes sweetheart I did, but I didn't recognize him... Did you, Doug?" Doug would shake his head and then excuse himself to the back porch. He would light a Camel and take a long, hard drag. He would blow streams of smoke from his nose and remember the way I used to love when he did that. "Can you breathe fire, too?" I had said. "Of course," he had answered, "all dragons can." "So you admit it," I had whispered. He smiled then. He would blow more smoke and remember the first time he kissed me in his and Abagail's coat closet. He would remember the way I ran my fingers around his streams and the way I looked at him. He would remember the way he took hold of my wrist, pinning me against the guest's coats at Abagail's 40th birthday party; the way his lips felt against mine, soft and warm and gentle and firm, the way I pulled him closer. He would remember finding me attractive when Abagail first introduced us in college, about wishing he had met me before her. I want him to think of the last decade of my life then, the way he cheated on his wife and I cheated on my best friend, the way we never got caught, the way his eyes widened when I told him that I would leave, that he should too, the way he said he couldn't do that to Abagail, the way I said what about me, the way I looked at him when I said he would have to choose, the way he looked at me when he said *her*. I want him to remember the last time I kissed him, how it felt as soft and warm and gentle and firm as the first time. Then he would think of the stranger my daughter asked about and remember the way he touched my hand, and how angry it made him, because he wanted to be able to touch me that way but couldn't. All he could do was blow smoke streams and think of dragons.

I want her to find her father last, sitting at the dining room table with a half empty bottle of Bru-

gal and ask if he saw the man in the brown jacket and black fedora with a red feather. He would
stop pouring his rum and glance at her, "Yes." She
would wait for him to go on, and when he didn't,
she would ask, "Do you know him?" He would
continue filling his glass, "Why?" She would
say, "I've just never seen him before, wondered
how he knew Mom..." He would take a sip and
say what he knew he shouldn't, but because he is
who he is, he would, "He was her first lover." My
daughter would frown, "What?" He would repeat
himself, "He was her first lover." Then he would
smile, "Gotcha!" He would let out an echoing belly laugh that would ring through the house and
make everyone that heard it uncomfortable. She
would look at him in disgust and leave the table.
He would pick up the glass, feel its cold against
his fingers and he would remember the time he
picked up that old lead pipe. When he took it to
his younger sister's teacher after his sister told
him what the teacher had been doing to her. He
would remember striking the man thirteen times,
a good strong blow for every year his sister had
been his sister, being hauled off to juvy in his last
year of high school, not getting many visitors until
I came, how shocked he was to see me because we
never spoke at school, the way I took his hand and
said, "You did the right thing." He would remem-

ber thinking that was no way to start a healthy relationship, that it was just the thrill of it, but not acting on it, and instead saying, "You're the most beautiful thing I've ever seen." He would remember how we got married as soon as he got out of prison and I finished college, how I would parade him around and the looks people gave him. He'd remember how proud he was when he told me he finally found a trade, the way I forced a grin he knew to be fake because it looked nothing like the first day I went to see him in jail. I want him to rub his fingers against the cool glass and remember how disappointed I was when I realized he was just a boring man with a moral fiber that made him violent that one time, to remember the way I would provoke him, try and bring the boy with the lead pipe to the surface, when he knew that he would never be enough for me when I realized that boy wasn't coming back.

I want her to go to the bathroom and lock the door behind her, to splash her face a few times, to bend over the sink and feel her eyes begin to swell. I don't want her to think of the time I bent her over that same sink and stuffed a bar of Ivory into her mouth because she repeated *shit* after hearing me say it, or the time I laughed and told her not complain about constipation, that it hurt more going in then coming out, or her eighth birthday when she saw Mr. Whoever from up the street follow me into the bathroom and not retreat in embarrassment, or when I was gone the summer her period started, how she figured out what to do without me, or when she brought her first boy home and blushed when I whispered for her to open the top two buttons on her blouse. Instead, I want her to stand in the bathroom and remember my laugh, the way it made her smile, to think of how much my laugh reminded her of her own, that she loved that it did, to look up and stare into the mirror, to stare long and hard and she would examine her face, her high cheekbones and strong jaw, not so smooth skin and mildly tempered eyes. I want the thought to cross her mind, but only for second.

MONKEY PAWS

Alfred and Win have been together for six years.
Win wants to get married. Alfred does not. Alfred
wants a child. Win does not. But Alfred does not
want six years to feel like an utter waste of time.
Neither does Win. So, Win stays with Alfred. And
Alfred stays with Win.

This reality frustrates Alfred. Although, it
does not deter him from his wish. Alfred sought
a child, so he began his research. A human child
would require too much space, as they grow to be
far too big, so he moved on to the next best thing.
After months of web-searching and discovering
that his idea was legal in the place he lived, Alfred
found him. He found his child. Alfred knew his
name immediately, the name he would give his
son. Samson. He remembered the story of Samson
from the Bible, even though he didn't believe in

it and was raised Buddhist. He remembered that Samson's strength was bred of his hair. That it encapsulated his power and made him fiercer than anyone could imagine. This little guy on the web had some serious hair. So it fit.

The site's contact informed Alfred that the process might take a little while, and that he should use the time to prepare for his new arrival. There was a list:

Diapers
Fresh and dried fruit
Flea and tick shampoo
Living facility
High thread count sheets
Seeds and biscuits
Toys
Purified water

And much more. The contact also informed Alfred that this would be close to a lifelong commitment. He would require far more attention and care than a dog or cat would. Finally, the contact told him that before making the final payment, Alfred needed to be sure he was ready for this. Without hesitation, he forwarded the payment for Samson.

It was only after this that he realized his dilem-

ma, he had nowhere to store Samson's belongings. Nowhere to store them that Win wouldn't
see. Unless...

Alfred began tiptoeing around the old house he
and Win purchased the year before. Win thought
the house was filled with character, and Alfred
thought it was filled with creaky wood and damp
walls. Alfred found himself on the second floor,
staring upwards at a box on the ceiling. They had
an attic, and Win was terrified of dark and con-
fined spaces; he got stuffed into too many lockers
as a kid, it made him claustrophobic. Alfred made
a joke once that had it not been for a bunch of ho-
mophob*ic* teens, Win wouldn't have picked up
his *'ic'* affliction. Win didn't find it funny. Alfred
grabbed the dangling rope and pulled down. He
climbed into the attic and was overwhelmed by
the dust. It occurred to him that neither he nor Win
had ever been up there. It was spacious. About as
big as their room and the spare. The walls were
grey and water damaged, but the window, the
window was beautiful. Bright stained glass that
acted as a conversation piece before people even
entered the house. It might have been the only
thing Alfred and Win agreed on about the house,
it was a beautiful. After a good cleaning—they
were too frightened to clean the window out of
fear that it'd shatter into a thousand tiny pieces—

this would be ideal. The attic would be Samson's. Samson's and Alfred's.

Alfred was in IT and worked from home. Win was in medicine and was often gone. It was a flawless arrangement. Alfred could spend his days at home with Samson and have him tucked away in the attic by the time Win was home in the late evening. Alfred began preparing by buying a slew of cleaning products. From scrubs, to floor polishes, dusters, and sprays—he wanted the attic to be spotless. He cleaned every day for a week, before he began compiling everything Samson would need. He hired two men to assist him in the building and loading of supplies. They were the first two to respond to his ad on craigslist, Alfred had no time to be picky.

> *In need of two temporary employees for two to three days of work. Previous home and handy work experience preferred. Must be able to lift upwards of 60 pounds and be discreet in handling the assigned projects – $80/day.*

Their names were Rahul and Bill.

The mini-fridge went up first. It took all three of them to finagle it through the narrow, almost crooked, entry way. The materials for Samson's little house went up next, to call it a cage seemed barbaric. It came in so many pieces Alfred thought it might take an extra person to put it together before Win got home, but Rahul and Bill managed. Over the next few days they brought up the rest of Samson's belongings; boxes of food, toys, linen, changing tables, diapers, artwork, shelves, the indoor climbing frame, and everything else. They brought them up and began putting the room together. By the third day, they'd done all of the big work, Alfred could handle the rest on his own. The last thing he had Rahul do was install a lock on the attic entrance, Alfred had the only two keys.

The next few weeks were whirlwinds of organizing and sorting and storing, and every night before 7:00pm, Alfred would lock up and meet Win downstairs. Win picked up dinner—neither knew or cared to learn how to utilize the kitchen—from a new Mom and Pop he discovered, a Ukrainian spot. Neither had had Ukrainian food before.

"Chicken Kiev and Pirozhki," Win announced as he started unpacking the bag.

"I thought Pirozhki was a Russian thing," Alfred said. "I've had it before, at a Russian restaurant, I think it's closed down now."

Win didn't respond.

"You okay?" Alfred asked.

"We both grew up eating buns, right?" Win suddenly questioned.

"Yeah..."

"Our parents are from different countries in Asia, does that mean one of us is lying. That buns can only exist in one place?"

Alfred exhaled, "I was just making conversation Wi-"

"No you weren't," Win interrupted. "You always do that... like things are just one way or the other."

Alfred looked at Win and wondered if he knew. If his secret wasn't so secret after all.

"Where's this coming from?" Alfred asked.

Win shook his head, "The same place it always does."

They stopped talking, finished their meal, and went to bed. The next morning Alfred received the email he'd been waiting for, Samson would be there by the end of the week. Alfred's glee was so vast and bright Win saw it all over him, but he didn't ask about it, what made him that happy.

Friday came in a blink, and so did Alfred's delivery. The doorbell rang at 12:58pm. Alfred knew it as an early sign of good fortune. He caught himself with the thought as he approached the door and was immediately reminded of his father, which frightened more than elated him. Alfred opened the door and signed for the large Styrofoam container with air holes on his porch. He gently cradled the box and slowly began carrying it towards the attic. Alfred expected the box to be shifting, for little Samson to be rattling around, scared or curious, but he was as still as the box he was packaged in. Unnerved and unmoved. It wasn't how Alfred pictured it, he thought Samson would be being carried by a young woman with kind eyes that told him this was his new home. No such luck.

Alfred unlocked the attic door and shifted the container up the ladder. He placed the box on the small play table and retrieved a pair of scissors. The anticipation was growing deeply within Alfred, with every trace of the scissors his palms would tremble and the hairs on his toes would curl under themselves. Soon there was nothing keeping the lid tied down. Alfred wrapped his fingers around the edges and took a deep breath. Alfred removed the lid.

There he was. No more than fifteen pounds, lying flat on his back, sleeping soundly. His little fingers balled together in tight fists and his toes facing the ceiling. Alfred watched as his tiny lungs filled and emptied and filled and emptied.

He wanted to cry, but refused. That was the last way he thought Samson should be introduced to him. Alfred carefully placed his middle and index finger on Samson's rising and falling stomach, just above his belly button. Alfred slowed his breathing then. Long inhales of partially humid air filling his lungs in almost tedious increments, but it was working. Alfred managed to mimic Samson's pattern, every time he inhaled, Alfred did, every time Alfred exhaled, Samson did. It was like nothing Alfred had experienced before. He loved him already, and couldn't explain it, but realized he didn't have to.

Samson began to squirm as Alfred rubbed his fingers along his long healthy hair, and soon he opened his eyes. Brown and full and wet, Alfred could see himself, clear as day, in Samson's eyes, so he knew Samson could see him, just as clearly. Alfred tucked his hand under Samson's neck and the back of his head, slowly lifting him up. He placed Samson next to his heart, his small ear laid flat against Alfred's chest; he wondered if Samson could hear it, the way their hearts were beating in unison. Alfred watched as Samson opened his fist and reached out before he grabbed hold of Alfred's thumb and squeezed it as though they'd met before, like they were old friends. Alfred closed his eyes and sat down in the rocking chair the two men put together for him, and he swayed, back and forth, until both he and Samson fell into the dream that was now a reality.

Alfred's morning routine went like this: wait for Win to leave a few minutes before 7:00am, head into the attic, unlock Samson's home and greet him with a hug and kiss, go to the changing table and get a new nappy on, set Samson on his climber, let him explore, grab fresh berries and bananas from the mini fridge, mash them into a paste, add apricots sometimes — Samson loved them — feed Samson his breakfast, if he was still hungry, warm, give him half a bottle of milk, and sit in the rocker. They'd done this every morning for a few weeks, and Samson was already growing. He managed his way through the climber, not the highest ceiling bars though, without Alfred's help anymore, it was slow, but he managed. He was already so independent, Alfred thought.

Alfred would spend most days working in the attic with Samson, he mostly played, and pooped, and ate, and slept. There were times when Alfred had to leave during the day, a meeting or fruit run, and he would look up at the stained-glass attic window. He always hoped to see Samson's face pressed against it, watching him, missing him. Samson was never there. Too busy playing, climbing, Alfred figured, or snacking on biscuits and milk. Then, whenever he'd return, he'd glance up at the window, in hopes that Samson would be waiting for him to hurry back. Still, Samson was never there.

Samson was a quiet little thing, rarely made a peep. Never once made a sound when Win was home and Alfred had locked him in his house for the night. He'd roll over with his stuffed elephant, BeeBop, and go right to bed; they needed lots of rest. During the day, he'd sit on Alfred's lap and fall off to sleep at least twice but didn't require much else save feeding and cleaning. Samson loved bath time. He'd grab at the suds like they were clouds and he was determined to climb towards the sun. Alfred would laugh, they'd both laugh. Alfred would sometimes style Samson's hair with the suds, give him Mohawks and pompadours, and he'd look up at him with those big brown eyes. Alfred desperately wanted to take a picture, to have times like these at his fingertips. Not with Win knowing his passcode though, but how Alfred longed to snap a pic and post it online... how he wanted the world to see how perfect Samson was.

It had been just over a month since Samson had arrived when Win planned an impromptu dinner date with Alfred.

"We never spend any time together," Win said as they drove home from the dive bar he took Alfred to. "Wasn't this nice?"

Alfred took Win's hand, "It was."

The two smiled at each other before Win kissed Alfred's hand. Then Win became tense, Alfred felt it in his palm, the sudden rigidness in his fingers.

Win spoke softly, "Oh, I completely forgot to mention..."

Win hesitated, so Alfred chimed it, "Mention what?"

Win said, "Connie's going to be staying with us for a while."

Alfred looked straight ahead and pulled his hand away from Win.

"So that's what tonight was," Alfred said. "A way to butter me for this?"

Win said, "I shouldn't have to butter you up, she's my sister."

"And a pain in the ass," Alfred regretted it the moment it left his lips, but it was too late now, and he meant what he said.

Connie was twenty four, entitled, picky, brash, rude, and just horrid in general. Alfred once thought of telling Win that one of the reasons he didn't want to marry him was because he didn't want Connie for a sister-in-law. It was mostly out of anger, but a small portion of it was the truth, so he decided to keep it to himself, plus, that would mean a more in-depth conversation about why Alfred seemed to have an aversion to marriage. Which would lead to why Win didn't want children, and those arguments were messy, so Alfred kept his trap shut.

Win swerved the car over to a barren lot. He peered at Alfred, Alfred said nothing.

"You will not talk about my family that way," Win raised his voice. "Ever, again."

"I'm sorry," Alfred whispered.

Win snapped back, "No you're not."

"You're right," Alfred agreed before he turned and faced Win. "When's she coming?"

Win was furious, he pulled off faster than Alfred liked, "She's already here."

They arrived home to an exhausted Connie laid out on the front porch, more bags than Alfred felt comfortable with her having.

"What took you so long?" Connie asked her brother.

"You said you'd be here at eleven," Win smiled. "It's 11:12!"

Win hugged her and Alfred pulled out his keys.

"Hey to you too, Alfred," Connie said.

"Hey," Alfred muttered.

He opened the door and grabbed her bags. Alfred headed upstairs with Connie's things and piled them inside the guest room. He got clean linen and towels. The siblings were sipping wine when Alfred joined them in the kitchen.

"Connie's painting now," Win said to Alfred, as though he'd care.

"Hmm," Alfred nodded, pouring himself a glass of red.

Connie chimed in, "I'm experimenting with oils, really prefer them to acrylic and water."

Alfred said nothing, only sipped his wine.

"I was thinking," Connie went on. "I should set up a little artist corner while I'm here. Treat it like a retreat..."

Alfred blew and Win gave him a look.

"My room's a bit small," Connie concluded.

"You mean the guest room?" Alfred asked.

Connie only glanced at Alfred, "Is there another space I can paint in, Win?"

Win, still eyeing Alfred, replied, "I'm not sure, babe, we use a lot for storage... Well, there's the attic."

Alfred's heart stopped. The wine nearly down his throat came to a complete halt, like it heard what Win said as well, prompting Alfred to cough, ferociously. As he coughed his eyes became pink and inflamed, red wine seeping from the sides of his mouth.

"You okay?" Win stood and walked over to Alfred.

Alfred replied as he felt Win's hand pat his back, "Fine, just went down the wrong way."

He coughed softly then, Win's pat shifting into a rub as he looked deeply at Alfred, silently gesturing, *you sure?* It warmed Alfred, his touch, he forgot how much so. It was little moments, like this and in the morning when Win thought Alfred was asleep and would adjust Alfred's sheets to just below his neck, where Alfred liked them, but Alfred wouldn't be sleeping, but waiting for Win to leave so that he could wake Samson and tell him he loved him. It was always in the little moments. Alfred nodded and grinned, squeezing Win's hand against his shoulder.

"An attic," Connie spoke loudly. "That could work. I'll check it out in the morning, I'm gonna crash."

Connie gave herself a top up and went to bed. Win went shortly after. When the house was quiet, Alfred felt his panic returning. He unlocked the attic and slipped inside. Samson was asleep, curled up next to Beebop under his Magic School Bus sheets. He looked so peaceful there. Samson slept as though the world were a safe place. His breathing as steadied as the first time Alfred saw him. Alfred loved watching him sleep. He unlocked the little door and rubbed the side of Samson's face. Samson started to stretch and coolly opened his eyes. He reached up for Alfred, arms wide, but Alfred didn't pick him up. He only watched him, arms hovered, eyes still opening. He watched him and rubbed his silky cheek. Alfred didn't know what to do.

Alfred got up as soon as Win left the next morning, Connie was still knocked out. He fed and bathed Samson before locking the attic and retreating to his bedroom. He heard Connie fumbling around in the bathroom before making her way into the kitchen and then back upstairs. It was quiet for a while, then Alfred heard some fiddling in the hall, before he heard the footsteps, and the knock.

Connie cracked the bedroom door, "Hey, where's the key for the attic?"

Alfred hesitated, "Key?"

Connie opened the door the rest of the way, "Yeah, there a huge friggin' padlock up there. Where's the key?"

Alfred shrugged, barely glancing up from his laptop. Connie pulled out her cell and closed the door. Alfred could hear her on the phone with Win, and knew in less than a minute he'd be on the phone with him. Alfred didn't think about what he'd say about the lock, how and when it got there, if he'd pretend to not know of its existence, he didn't think of ignoring the call and not dealing with it until Win got home, and he didn't even think of Samson upstairs staring at the entry wondering what the strange sounds of Connie pulling on the lock were; instead, he thought about that story again, of Samson and Delilah. He thought of Samson's hair, the source of his great strength, and he thought of Delilah, the woman that took it all away. Alfred heard Connie get off the phone, moments before his started to ring.

"Hello," Alfred answered.

"Hey," Win said. "Why's there a lock on the attic?"

Alfred replied, "Don't know, must have always been there..."

"I don't remember there being one up there."

"You don't remember what you ordered for dinner last night," Alfred forced a chuckle.

Win laughed.

"There has to be a key," Alfred said. "I'll look around."

"Okay," Win said. "Let me know if you can't find it, I'll call a locksmith or something."

Alfred paused, "No need for that, I'll take care

of it."

Alfred was short of breath as he hung up. He stood, about to head upstairs to be with Samson, but heard Connie, still fiddling. Alfred backed up into his bed and covered himself in the sheets. He felt like the ceiling was caving in on him; that Samson grew to be the size of King Kong and was falling through the roof, flat on his father, on the only thing that loved him. Alfred stayed in his room all day, under the sheets for most of it. Connie was bustling around the house, looking for the key in Alfred's pocket he presumed. She'd called to him from the hall a few times, inquiring about the key. *Not yet*, he'd say, *not yet*.

Win brought dinner home and the three sat down.

"Connie said neither of you had any luck," Win went on. "I still don't remember there being a lock on that thing."

"Actually," Alfred said. "I thought about it, why don't we clear out the shed for you Connie?"

Connie looked at Alfred, "Why?"

Alfred cringed before he said, "There's a bit more privacy out there, and since you said you wanted it to feel like a retreat—I thought that'd be a good option."

Connie placed her fork in the plate, "It's hot outside."

Alfred glanced at Win, who was avoiding him all together.

"Well," Alfred said. "Heat rises, Connie, so it's probably just as hot, or worse, up there."

"You have central AC," she responded without hesitation. "The attic will be fine…"

Alfred looked at Win again, who still wouldn't look at him. Alfred didn't respond to Connie. He cleared his plate and grabbed his keys.

Win asked, finally acknowledging him, "Where are you going?"

"Grocery store," Alfred said as he reached for the front door.

"Wait for me," Connie stood and ran down behind him. "I need a grab a few things."

Alfred's eyes rolled so far back in his head only the whites were visible. They went to the market and Connie looked for her green juice ingredients, Alfred picked up a few varieties of dried apricots and mangos. Waiting in line at the register, Alfred felt a tap on his back. He faced the man and didn't recognize him at first, but was quickly washed over by the memory. Bill. It was Bill.

"Hey man," Bill said. "Longtime."

"Yeah," Alfred whispered, attempting to stand in Connie's line of sight.

"That your wife," Bill asked. "The little one

here yet?"

Alfred shook his head and sensed Connie's attention focus in on Bill as the cashier rang them up. Bill picked up on the tension and left with a slight gesture and nod.

"Who was that?" Connie asked.

"Guy I used to work with…"

"What was he talking about?"

"I don't know Connie, let's go." Alfred grabbed their bags and headed for the car.

Connie inquired about Bill the entire way home, where they worked, when he knew him, what he said. Alfred didn't remember most of his answers, everything started running together. When they got home Win was already in bed, so Connie turned in as well. A few hours later Alfred snuck into the attic. Samson was balled up in the rocking chair, Alfred didn't get a chance to put him to bed that night. Alfred picked him up and held him before sitting. Seeing Bill confirmed what Alfred had been thinking, been knowing. The little one was here, and he needed to be the priority. Alfred was so tired.

"We're leaving this place Samson," Alfred whispered. "Just me and you."

Samson buried his head into the soft spot between Alfred's ribs and bicep, grabbing hold of his t-shirt before falling back to sleep. Alfred began to cry then, he wasn't sure why, the inclination just touched him. He closed his eyes and cried as he rocked Samson and ran his hands across his deep black hair.

"Just me and you," Alfred said as a wave of sleep flooded him as quickly as the tears did. "And we'll be happy."

Alfred wasn't sure if it was the light from the stain glass window or the sound of Win's voice that woke him, but when he opened his eyes, there they were; Connie and Win in the attic. Samson was nowhere to be seen.

"Al," Win knelt down beside him. "What the hell is this?"

"Where's Samson," Alfred slowly stood. "Where is he?"

"Who the fuck is Samson?" Connie asked.

"Shhh," Win hushed his sister. "What is all of this?"

"Where's Samson?" Alfred raised his voice and began looking around.

No one responded. Alfred hurried to Samson's climber, to his little house, then under the play table. While Alfred searched, so did Win. He walked around the room and took in every detail, every fallen or loose toy, every intricacy. In their searches, both noticed each other across the room, their eyes met in furies of confusion and fear. Alfred saw Win's confusion, and Win saw Alfred's fear.

"Explain," Win said.

"No," Alfred replied, shifting his gaze towards Connie. "Tell me what you did with Samson."

"What are you talking about?" Connie asked.

"Who is Samson?" Win questioned as he stepped closer to him.

Alfred rubbed his shoulder and looked around, "He's my... my..."

"What?!" Connie said abruptly.

Alfred's palms moistened as the air in the room seemed to thin. He looked from Win to Connie and back to Win. He wasn't sure what to say. The seconds were beginning to draw out as Alfred ran through all the possible answers to their question. *My son.* No, that wouldn't sound right. It did to Alfred, but he knew it wouldn't to them. *My pet.* No, he couldn't say that. Not about Samson. Alfred felt Win growing anxious as Connie's eye's widened and she mouthed some inaudible vulgarity to her brother. Alfred had to say something. For the first time, Alfred had to say something about Samson.

"My chimp!" Alfred said.

"Your chimp?" Win asked.

Alfred nodded, "I got him about a month ago, and I've been keeping him up here. I got the mini-fridge brought up by a couple of guys, they built his cage and climber too, but I did most of the rest myself. I get him his special shampoos, biscuits and fruit, anything he needs."

Win and Connie looked around the room and then back at Alfred.

"Where is he?" Alfred begged. "Just tell me what you did with him."

"Al," Win was directly in front of him now. "That's not a cage, it's a crib..."

Alfred saw Win's expression change. Where confusion became concern.

"What?" Alfred asked.

Win walked to the other side of the room and touched Samson's house, "This is a crib. Not a cage."

As Win's fingers ran across the edge of the cage, the thin metal bars transformed into solid white wood. The cage door was gone and instead Alfred saw ornately crafted fixtures on each of the crib's corners. He stared at the crib as he approached it.

"But—"

"And is this what you're calling a climber?" Connie interrupted as she pointed at the ceiling. "These are mobiles, a shit tone of them, but they're mobiles."

Alfred looked up and the climber was gone, but there were at least twenty five baby mobiles hanging from the ceiling; singing yellow school buses, purple elephants, and little beige monkeys dancing around in circles.

"But he was here," Alfred affirmed. "I fed him, bathed him..."

"With what, Johnson and Johnson?" Connie raised her eyebrow. "Your crazy ass needs to get some help. Building a god damn nursery like an expecting—"

Connie dropped the bottle of baby wash and mumbled to herself as she left the attic at a calm, leisurely pace.

"He ate so much, Win," Alfred swore down. "Dried apricots were his favorite."

Win forced a soft grin before he opened the mini fridge, "There's just formula in here."

Alfred didn't look, he couldn't look. He walked around the room that all of a sudden looked completely different. The toys were the same, so was the rocker and the sheets, even the play table, but every sign of him was nonexistent. Everything Samson loved, was gone. Alfred walked and continued to search.

Win whispered, "Alfred-"

"There!" Alfred almost shouted. "On the window. Can you see it?"

Alfred ran towards the stain glassed window and pressed his face next to it.

"See what?" Win questioned.

"His little paw prints," Alfred said. "They're right here, in the glass. Look."

Win didn't move, and Alfred didn't look back at him. He gazed at the little prints left behind, wanting to touch them, but afraid he might wipe them away.

"Do monkeys have paws, or hands?" Alfred asked as he marveled at the only piece of Samson the room seemed to have left. "They look so much like ours."

Maybe Eighteen, Maybe Dudley, or Maybe the Dragon

The first time she saw it was at 3:52am, not because she enjoyed pacing outdoors in the moonlight, but because Dudley had to piss. He'd been going all over the apartment since they moved in a few weeks ago, so when he came clamoring, Shell forced herself out of bed and onto the porch. That's where she saw it—the eighteen-wheeler parked outside the complex, directly in front of her place. Well, as directly as a 60-foot truck could be in front of a single apartment.

There were no identifying marks on the vehicle, no brandings or logos, and in all honesty, she wasn't quite sure why she was looking for any. Like most of her neighbors, she'd usually be asleep and blissfully unaware of the eyesore, but she wasn't that morning, and was very aware. The truck was parked near the edge of the sidewalk, its tires neatly tucked inches from the curb. It was too big for the petite parking lot, Shell's mini coop was almost too big, so it straddled the entrance and blocked it instead.

Shell looked around as Dudley ran leash-less from tree to tree in the complex's common yard, wondering what the hell sort of delivery was being made. She readjusted her ponytail as the thick mane of curls mostly tussled in front of her face, no longer tied together by the rope of a hair-tie she used to reel it in. "Bedhead," she whispered to herself, suddenly craving a smoke. She'd been off them since she left Warren a month or so ago, she decided to quit all her bad habits at once. She couldn't deal with the patch's nausea, so she chewed the gum, vigorously. Maybe it was the night air. Maybe it was the night loneliness, in the past she would have been paired with a lit cigarette and maybe another smoker. Or maybe it was just hard to break a habit, a long-standing habit.

Shell whistled for Dudley and he came scurrying back. She looked at the truck and thought about a scene from *Goodfellas*, the one where Henry lifts the truck outside the diner. *That sort of delivery?* She was sure her mind went there because she'd watched the crime drama a couple of nights ago, but who's to know. She let Dudley in first and followed closely behind. She fumbled through her purse before going back to the bed-room and pulled out a couple pieces of Nicorette. She put a piece on each side of her jaw and began to chew, one was orange and the other cherry. The flavor didn't last long, but Shell didn't need it to. She just needed a hit of nicotine, and once she got it, all was well. She was about to make her way to the bedroom, when she heard another door shut.

Shell went for the blinds and glanced between the turned-up edges. A man was walking past with a hundred-key keychain dangling from the back of his jeans. He was lighting up as he walked past Shell's apartment, and once he did, he readjusted the plain white tee he wore the way we adjust ourselves after getting dressed. *Oh,* she thought, *that sort of delivery.* The line's taw-driness was enough to make her chuckle, and she watched the truck driver get in and go. Shell thought about her neighbor then, as she was sure he came from her apartment. Jessica was a plump red head, eighteen or nineteen years-old at most, that moved in a month or so before Shell. They'd spoken in passing a few times; she was in culinary school and wanted to be a pastry chef.

"My dad always loved my baking, mom not so much," Jessica had said. "She was always on some low carb thing."

"Aren't we all," Shell had said.

She didn't seem the type, Shell thought as she forced her foot against Dudley, keeping him from following her in the bedroom. He was a Border Collie sheep-dog mix; he shed too much. Jessica didn't seem the type to entertain 4:00amers, but *Who was?* she questioned while slipping under the sheets. The type that partakes in booty calls, knowingly or unknowingly, she supposed. Though she found it extremely difficult to believe it could truly go unknown.

Dudley kept the same clamoring up for the next few nights, just minutes to four, and she would hear him. Shell didn't see the truck for a couple of days, though. Maybe it was a one-night-stand. Their routine stayed consistent on the third day as well, Shell getting ready for work, she was in retail sales, ignoring at least three of Warren's calls, taking Dudley for a walk when she got home, falling asleep, and being awoken by Dudley in the wee hours.

She let him outside and there it was, the eighteen-wheeler. Parked in exactly the same place it was before. Shell leaned against the porch column, paying more attention to the truck than Dudley, when a door shut closed and scared her much more than her reaction revealed. She immediately looked next door and saw the man coming from Jessica's apartment, he looked directly at her. Shell turned away as the man stepped onto the walkway. She expected him to keep going, to get in go, but he stopped. He stopped directly in front of Shell's porch.

"What's his name?" The man asked, motioning to the returning dog.

"Dudley," Shell responded.

He knelt down and rubbed him all over — behind the ears, head, back, and tummy. He even let Dudley's slobber dribble on his hands. He was a dog person.

"That's an interesting name." He looked up at Shell.

"It's after the dragon," Shell uttered before it was too late to take back.

The show came out when she was thirteen, *Dudley the Dragon*, and quickly became her guilty pleasure — she still hummed the theme song in the shower. She watched it the entire three years it aired, yes; she was the sixteen-year-old rushing home for a public access preschool show. She never told anyone. There was something about that mindless dragon that interested Shell, something pure, innocent if you would; a coy sweetness in his should-have-been ferocious veracity. She knew even then she didn't want kids, too much pressure, so she decided that when she adopted her first puppy, she'd name it Dudley. That didn't exactly pan out as the first two were female, but the third wasn't.

He raised his eyebrow a bit when Shell explained, "It was a show in the nineties..."

"I don't think I know that one," he stood up and extended his hand. "I'm Carl, by the way."

Shell's eyes narrowed before she reciprocated, "Shell."

"That short for something?"

The question was so common to her she didn't have the energy to get annoyed by it anymore.

"Nope," she shrugged. "Just, Shell."

Carl smiled and stuffed his hands in his pockets. It was then that Shell noticed he was cute, in a balding early forties kind of way. He was tall, six one, six two maybe, and slender, besides the budding beer belly. Clear brown eyes and nice skin, but that smile, that smile is probably what got him in next door. She glanced at his wedding band last. *Jeez*, she thought. If he was bold enough to wear his ring to the other women's apartment, what would stop Warren. He had no ring. Shell wanted no ring.

"You like dogs," Shell asked Carl.

"Yeah, never had one though," he replied. "You clearly do."

"Always liked 'em," Shell said. "When you tell

them to *stay*, they stay, you say *come*, and they come. Say *stop*, they stop."

"Not all dogs, I'm sure."

"Mine do," she said.

"Sounds like you like obedience, loyalty even. Not dogs, necessarily," Carl said, pulling his hand from his pocket.

Shell shrugged, "They'll do."

Carl laughed, so did Shell.

"You want a smoke?" Carl tilted the pack towards her.

She yearned for one, for the burning throat and smoky nostrils, just to feel one between her lips, but she shook her head, "I quit."

"Oh," Carl nodded, unsure if he should take one out or not.

"It's no problem," she motioned to the box of Camels. "Go ahead. I was a Marlboro girl anyway."

He grinned, placing a cigarette between his teeth, "Right."

Smoking was Shell's vice and had been since she was eighteen. It didn't bother her much though; it seemed a family tradition, not smoking, vices. Her father was a drunk and a cheat, and her mother a compulsive gambler, not the casino kind, the lottery ticket kind. She'd spend entire paychecks on them, max out credit cards, and borrow from neighbors, uncles, and Toms. That's why her father left, or so he said. Shell always figured it was more about the booze than her mother, if she was sucking them dry with her gambling, he couldn't be with his drinking. He married his mistress a few months later, and his vice persevered. So did her mother's.

Shell hadn't spoken to her father in nearly two decades, not because of something he did, more like something he didn't do. On one of her bi-annual weekend visits this one Easter, Shell overheard an argument between her father and stepmother; the walls were paper thin. The stepmother was complaining about the ex, Shell's mother, something Shell figured a commonality amongst most second wives. She complained about the child support not supporting the child, and them having to pick up the slack. Shell assumed she was referring to the recent wisdom tooth extraction she'd undergone. Then she said it, the word no teenager needs to hear her father's new white wife say about his ex-black wife. Shell heard the N sound roll off her tongue so comfortably, she knew it couldn't have been the first time she said it. She waited for her father to say something, to snap the way he would when her mother couldn't pay the bills and the hot water was out, or there was no food in the kitchen, but he didn't. He didn't. Twenty minutes later she heard their bed screeching a slow steady beat, it only lasted ten minutes or so. The walls were so paper-thin.

The next morning, she left without a word. She thought about leaving a note, even picked up a pen, but when she saw her father's chicken scratch on top of the pad, she didn't bother; *white potatoes and spinach* was what it said. Maybe it was because she looked more like him than her mother, Shell tried to figure it out on the way home. Maybe it was because her hair was the only give away that she wasn't as blue-blooded as her blue-eyed father, maybe that's why he didn't say anything. Or maybe it was because he couldn't squander his meal ticket, the enabler that kept him a functioning alcoholic for another two decades; maybe it was because her father was just that much of an ass. He called sometimes, usually on one of those bi-annual visits Shell didn't show up for, still does, and she still doesn't answer. She started smoking a few months later.

Shell continued to look at Carl's truck, and when she glanced back at him she saw him staring at her breasts. She didn't have much, but she knew when someone was checking them out. She didn't take much offense, braless in spaghetti straps with a soft chill; she might have been more insulted if he didn't look. He averted his eyes instantly, as she changed the topic.

"Who do you drive for?" she asked him.

"Myself," he said. "Went independent six years ago."

"You prefer it that way, huh?"

"Oh yeah," he nodded. "Doesn't everyone want to be their own boss?"

Shell tilted her head, "Not everyone."

Carl nodded, "I guess."

Shell felt him watching her, hard. She was prettier than Jessica, Shell thought. Not sure why she thought it. She was a good bit older, not quite twenty years, but she was prettier. Shell imagined she and Carl were about five or so years apart.

"Well, I gotta run," he said. "Maybe I'll see you next time I'm in town."

Shell grinned then whistled for Dudley, who'd departed again, "As long as he keeps waking me up, I'm sure you will."

Carl smiled that smile, and Shell followed Dudley inside. She went for the blinds a second later and watched him walk away. Shell wondered how Jessica met Carl, where and how the conversation even got started. She wondered who approached who, Carl no doubt. Why would an eighteen-year-old approach a balding truck driver? Maybe she did, maybe she was lonely living in a new city alone. Everyone gets lonely sometimes. Carl was in his truck then, he tossed the butt, and was gone.

Shell went into her room and saw a missed-call—it could only be one person at that time of the morning. Warren. They'd been on-again, off-again for four years, and the off-agains always stemmed in his being on some other young hotty, again. Warren was a looker, not like Carl, a real looker. Broad shoulders, in-shape, full lips, sultry eyes, and everything else you use to describe a hunk. If he'd set his mind to it, he could have been one of the few LA dreamers that made it, Shell told him that. But he said it wasn't practical, so he worked maintenance instead.

"Assholes come in every shape and color," her mother had said to her when she stayed there for a few weeks after leaving him. "As long as they got something between their legs, you'll find 'em—won't you?"

Shell bit her lip as her mother got cranked up. Race didn't matter to Shell, she'd dated every color under the sun. Size didn't matter much either; she did like them tall, though. She knew it bothered her mother, not that she dated different shades and shapes, but that she didn't have a type.

"What do you want in a man?" her mother

asked her. "Do you even know?"

The question went in one ear out the other but lingered long enough for Shell to consider it. And she would, eventually, but the only thing she knew at that moment was that she needed to get out of her mother's house. She did about a week later.

Shell didn't expect to see Carl the next night, or the night after. It seemed to be a three-day deliver route. Maybe she'd invite him in next time, for coffee. Maybe they would talk about something other than dogs, dragons, and drags over coffee, maybe not. Maybe they would talk about the person on the other end of that wedding band. Maybe he'd caress her shoulders and she'd tickle his beer belly. Maybe they'd talk about why he and Warren were such dogs, why so many of them were such lovely smiling, sparkly-eyed dogs. Or maybe they'd just talk about the coffee.

On the third night she thought she heard a knock, and then she was sure. Dudley was barking. Shell looked at the time, a few minutes after four. *Who...* she began to ask herself, but realized Dudley hadn't woken her up that morning. It was Carl, it had to be Carl. Shell jumped up, pulling the hair-tie all the way out then coiffing the freed curls. *Why am I jumping, primping?* She asked herself only for a moment, before she was twisting the knob. It wasn't who she expected. Not Carl with his warn out jeans, faded tee, wedding band, bald spot, and sweet smile; it was Warren with his... everything.

"What are you doing here?" she whispered.

"Can I come inside," he said.

"For what?" she asked.

"Please, Shell..."

She didn't want to, but a little piece of her melted when Warren said her name, just like it did the first time they met at her then apartment.

"Which sink is it?" he asked.

"The kitchen," she pointed towards the entrance.

He unclogged the drain and came back through the living room. Shell wondered if he'd noticed that she'd unzipped her hoody.

"Shouldn't give you any more problems," he winked. "If you need anything else, just ask for Warren."

"Will do," she blushed a bit.

She supposed he noticed that or wouldn't have had the gall to do what he did next.

"I didn't catch your name," Warren said.

I didn't throw it, was her usual comeback. Not this time, though.

"It's Shell," she said.

"Shell?" he replied as she waited for the inevitable follow up.

She nodded.

"That's a beautiful name," he smiled with his eyes, a concept Shell had heard but never understood until then.

Then he left. No questions about it being short form for Shelly or Michelle or Shelby. They went out a couple nights later.

Shell opened the door for Warren, peeking out over his shoulder. She didn't see it, the truck, it wasn't there.

"How'd you get my address?" Shell asked as she locked the door.

Warren rubbed Dudley's head, "I have my ways."

"What do you want, Warren?"

He looked up at her, eyes wide wet and full, "You know what I want."

Shell crossed her arms, "You have some damn nerve, you know."

Warren's strides were long and unyielding, as was the way his arms wrapped around Shell, making her feel so small and big and held, and the way his hands ran down her back and beneath her PJ bottoms, and the way he pulled her chest towards his, and the way he looked at her, and the way she tried to look away, and the way he looked at her, and the way she tried to pull back, and the way he wouldn't let her, and the way he looked at her. Shell uncrossed her arms then.

"What are we doing, babe?" Warren asked a few minutes after he had rolled off of her.

She put her cheek to his chest, "What do you mean?"

"You won't give me a baby, you won't even marry me," Warren whispered. "So what are we doing, Shell? What is this?"

"Love?" Shell asked more than stated.

"Are you shitting me," Warren sat up. "Why'd you leave?"

"You keep cheating on me, Warren."

"You keep taking me back, Shell."

She pulled away from him and rolled her eyes so far back they might have gotten stuck. Shell stretched out on her side of the bed with her back to Warren, saw Dudley's shadow under the door, and then she hummed. She hummed the theme song she'd been humming since she was thirteen years old so quietly Warren couldn't hear.

"Hello," Shell answered the phone the following morning, creeping out of the room.

"Good morning, you up?" her mother asked.

"I am now," Shell rubbed her eyes. "What's up, Ma?"

"Nothing much," her mother said. "I spoke to your daddy last night."

Shell didn't answer, and her mother didn't expect her to. She had stopped asking Shell if she'd talked to her father four years earlier. Shell's mother nearly begged her to tell her what happened between the two once, but she didn't, still hadn't. Shell didn't see the point, he'd caused her mother enough pain already.

"Said he and that heifer aren't getting along," her mother paused. "Asked if he could stay with one of us for a while an—"

"Why you lying?" Shell asked. "He didn't ask anything about staying with me. He asked if you would take him back, probably because his wife threw him out. And you said yes, didn't you?"

Her mother hesitated, "Well, I couldn't just let him sit in the street."

"Why the hell not," Shell said. "Didn't he leave you? Barely making it already, didn't he leave you?"

"Shell," her mother cleared her throat. "Your daddy always supported us, even when he went and remarried. He always took care of us, helped me out—"

"He wasn't there," Shell interrupted. "He didn't do shit!"

"You watch your nasty little mouth. You hear me," her mother snapped back.

They became quiet and the silence on the phone remained for another two minutes. Shell shook her head knowing her mother was too stubborn a woman to speak first.

"I hear you," Shell whispered again, this time with a slight laugh under her breath. "You never could pick a winner could you, Ma?"

"What did you say?" her mother said.

"Numbers, I mean. Numbers..." Shell hung up before her mother could speak, and she sent the next six calls her mother made straight to voicemail.

Shell didn't realize she was crying, not until Dudley came and nuzzled into her neck before licking her repetitively. She didn't feel a thing, the long streams flooding her face or the tightness in her throat. Dudley did though, he always did. She ran her fingers through his glossy fur and nuzzled him right back. Shell heard Warren stirring around the bedroom then jumped up and went to the bathroom. She wiped her face, then washed it, then wiped it again. She heard him come out of the room then, tip-toeing the way he would when he thought she was still asleep. She expected to hear him call her name then, to ask why she never had any good cereal, or where she kept the blender, but he didn't. Instead, she heard the front door close.

Shell stepped out of the bathroom. Dudley was waiting for her by the door. Maybe Warren had left for a tea run; he'd always get tea, and even though she preferred coffee, she'd drink it. Maybe he went to grab them a couple of McMuffins. Maybe he had to make a call — he took lots of calls outside — or needed to grab his charger. Or maybe Warren got what he came for and had gone home. When Shell looked out the blinds, his car was gone. She got a text a minute later — *gone 2 work, call you ;)*. She typed a response, short and quick. She thought about sending it but didn't bother. *You could have said goodbye.* She still loved him, and she didn't know what to do about it.

Shell didn't sleep that night; she sat up in the living room instead. She opened the blinds, slightly, and watched as Carl pulled in and meticulously parked in front of their lot. She watched him pass by, and unlock Jessica's door with his own key. Shell pulled out her phone then, and imagined the call she'd make; *Yes hi, there's a truck blocking my driveway and I have to get to work. I think I saw the guy go into my neighbor's place around 1:00am, but I don't feel comfortable knocking. Could you send someone out here?* How treacherous, she thought. Shell looked down at her phone then, she dialed the numbers slowly, 9-1-1, but she didn't bother to call. She nodded off half an hour later and stayed asleep until Jessica's door woke her three hours later. She thought about going to bed, about leaving Carl alone, but she opened the door instead.

"Hey Carl," Shell shouted before he got in the truck.

He smiled, "Hey, where's Dudley?"

Oh, she thought, *that's right—Dudley was still inside.*

"Sleeping," she said. "I'm the one that had to go tonight."

He chuckled.

"Can I bum a cigarette?" Shell asked.

"I thought you quit," he said handing her one.

"So did I," Shell replied.

"It's a bad habit," he said, both lighting up over his flame. "If you found a way to stop, maybe you should stick to it."

Shell took the longest drag of her thirty-five-year-old life. As she did, she stared at Carl's ring, at the way it shined with the tip of his cigarette. The way its hew made her think of Dudley's chest, stomach and neck—the dragon, not the dog. The way it resembled the one Warren offered to her three months earlier, when he'd probably been at some Jessica's apartment not but a few days before.

"Yeah, it's a bad habit... so is fucking a child," Shell said as she exhaled a stream of smoke and the words blew out as easily as it did. "How old is she, eighteen?"

Carl's eyes went cold, "What?"

Shell flipped her eyes at him. "I'm not your wife, okay. You can stop with the ignorant bull."

"Shell," Carl's voice softened a way Shell had never heard it. "Jessica is my daughter."

Her heart dropped, as low as humanly fathomable. It splattered all over the concrete and Shell had no idea how she was going to clean it all up.

"Oh my go-"

"It's alright," Carl interrupted. "I know how it looks."

Shell sucked the cigarette to calm her angst, only shrugging.

"She enjoys the company," Carl went on. "It's hard for her, being on her own like this. Changed my schedule around so I could spend nights with her, but mostly do it to see my girl between drop-offs."

"You don't have to explain," Shell said.

"Ah," Carl shrugged. "Good looking out, glad she has you."

Shell pressed her hand to her mouth and shook her head, because she didn't have her, there was no looking out, there was just Shell. The smoke between them thickened, Shell felt her pores absorbing the airy haze as Carl went on about truck routes and scheduling and pastries and dogs he never had and the daughter he did. Shell grinned, but mostly stayed for his second-hand smoke, first wasn't enough. They exchanged a few more nothings before she started dragging herself inside. But Shell stopped in front of her door, she couldn't help herself, he watched her too hard, too long. She stepped towards Carl.

"I can put a pot of coffee on," she said, smoke streaming from her nostrils.

His eyes flashed, Shell wasn't sure if it was eagerness or a hurried reflection of the moonlight. Maybe both. He wanted to say *yes, sure, yes, alright, yes, I have a few minutes, yes, yes, yes*; she saw it in those clear browns. But his smile, that smile, twisted into something else. Something she didn't recognize, didn't understand, didn't like. Carl looked away, gently fiddling with the band that reminded her of so much.

He whispered as if Jessica had her ear to the

door. "I'm married..."

Shell swallowed her smoke, a mouthful. She didn't cough.

She took a step back, "It was just coffee, Carl."

She didn't say goodbye, she only went inside.

She expected a call from Warren the next day, a call she'd ignore, roll her eyes at, maybe even curse about. But that call never came. She checked more than once, on her way to work, twice at lunch, once on break, and another time going home, but it never came. When Shell got to her apartment there was a package waiting for her with no return address. She brought it inside, and quickly tore whatever it was from its brown paper casing. It was light, she thought, but it was big, clunky even. As the paper cleared away Shell recognized the box and its occupant. *Odd*, she thought aloud. Shell opened the card next:

> *Found your address in Mom's book, thought you might still like this thing. Call me sometime, Shell. I love you, baby.*

This time Shell noticed everything — the tightness in her throat and welts of water forming in her ducts, the way her knees locked and fingers tensed as she brushed them against the dragon's green and yellow coloring, the way her heart raced and her mind took her back to that place, the screeching bed, N sound, and silence. The silence, his silence. How did he know? Shell pulled out her phone then, and imagined the call she'd make—How'd you know about the dragon? Did you know when he flew away, he'd always fly back? That he didn't blow smoke? Do you know I still can't stop humming his song? How'd you know about the dragon, dad? Tell me how you know?

Shell scrolled through her contacts and stared when she landed on her father's name. Her finger was against the call button, but she didn't bother. She shouldn't bother, couldn't bother. Shell wiped her flooded face as she watched the dragon, long and hard. She still loved him, and she didn't know what to do about it.

She took hold of the stuffed toy and carried it into her room. She sat on her bed, and then heard the pitter-patter at the door. She stood and opened it.

"Come on, Dudley," she said.

The dog tip-toed inside, weary of the place he had yet to see. She tapped the bed twice, and he jumped next her. Shell eased down on her side, both Dudleys snuggled in under each arm. Maybe it was the toy's new aroma, like cardboard and felt. Maybe it was the sound of Dudley's heartbeat nestled into to hers. Or maybe it was recalling that her father was the first person to call her "Baby," that she hadn't seen his hand writing since she was eighteen, and smoking, and furious, and searching, searching. She thought about her mother's question and mumbled her answer aloud.

"Yes, Ma," Shell squeezed the dragon and the dog, tightly. "I know."

Sonic Boom

They weren't friends, so Gayle wasn't sure why she was there. When Marge invited her to her family's beach house, Gayle was sure that the woman was talking to someone else.

"It'll be fun," Marge whispered as the women walked out of their Gen Ed class. "Everyone needs a vacation."

So, there they were, Gayle and Marge, classmates and utter strangers on their way to Marge's parents' third home, and Wilbur, Marge's so-old-he'd-cough-up-dust Labradoodle tied to the back seatbelt.

"This is the company car you know," Marge said as they turned off their last exit.

Gayle didn't respond, she wasn't sure how to. She knew Marge didn't work as she often bragged about the peace and quiet she lavished in while the kids were at school. So for a moment Gayle was fearful, fearful that she'd gotten into the car with a crazy woman driving her to rift-raft in her all-white, exterior and interior, BMW. At least she'd go in style.

"My father bought it for me two years ago," Marge concluded.

"I thought you said it was the company car," Gayle said.

Marge took a left at the light after they passed the town's military base, "It is! I take care of the estates for him, so he got me the car."

Gayle was over-inclined to roll her eyes, but she grinned and nodded, instead. Gayle and Marge were the same age, and the thought of her parents buying her a car in her late forties was almost laughable. They couldn't even buy her one in her teens. The comment began to resonate with Gayle though, as she remembered Marge mentioning why she was back in school on the first day of the semester. The group was all adult learners and they were asked to go around the circle to explain their reasons for returning.

"I always intended to get my BSN after finishing my nursing program, but after my twins were born I didn't have the time," Gayle went on. "It's just the three of us... The girls are in high school now, so Mama's back in school too!"

The class chuckled before the others started sharing; *better pay, need it for a promotion, on worker's comp and had the time*, and then there was Marge.

"I decided to come back and complete my degree in Accounting," that could have been the end of it, but as Gayle would learn, Marge had a tendency to put her foot in her mouth, and keep it there.

"It's not that I have to work or anything," Marge stressed. "My husband's a surgeon, so was my father, and my top priority is being there for him, my husband, and our three children—but now that Dad's retired he needs a bit of help with the books."

A couple of students in the circle shot eyes each other's way as Marge continued, "He has loads of investments—properties, stocks, you know—and it's getting to be a lot for him to handle. Not to mention I'm going to get it all, so I guess I need a refresher in dealing with finance."

Marge burst out into a wail of laughter, Gayle assumed the woman made a joke she wasn't privy to, but when the rest of the room sat as silently as she did, it was confirmed that the woman was laughing at her inheritance comment, and it was as awkward to everyone else as it was to Gayle.

Just like that, in a room full of worker bees, there was a queen.

Regardless of how off-putting the notion of Marge referring to the vehicle as a company car was, it was a welcome change in conversation as the rest of the trip had consisted of Marge talking about her husband, Brent.

"It used to be tough with him working such long hours, but he switched to the private sector about seven years ago and it's been great," Marge rambled. "The money is better too!"

Gayle mostly nodded as she couldn't get a word in edge-wise, but she didn't mind, Marge's chatter kept her from having to pretend that they actually had something in common.

Wilbur let out a muffled yelp and Gayle glanced at him; she'd almost forgotten he was back there. Marge stretched her long pale arm towards the dog, and he licked her fingers, meticulously.

"What's the matter, boy," Marge baby-talked. "We're almost there, you'll be out soon."

Gayle noticed the liver spots on Marge's fore-arm as she rubbed the dog's chin, it seemed she'd be too young for liver spots, Gayle always asso-ciated the markings with age. But much about Marge seemed too old for their age, the full head of grey curls, psoriatic arthritis, and already be-ing post-menopausal. That last fact was one Gayle

cringed at while listening to, as she finally understood her daughters' *TMI* reactions. Before their
third class together, Marge started venting about
how painful sex had become for she and her husband once she went through *the change*. How she
could discuss irritated vaginal walls with a virtual
stranger and not say 'menopause' was both dis-
tracting and comical.

"You can pet him if you'd like," Marge said.

Gayle shook her head, "I'm good."

She wasn't fond of dogs, and never had been.
Gayle didn't trust things she couldn't communi-
cate with that had the potential to harm either her,
or itself. She figured that was the reason for her
detachment from babies. She even felt impartial
about her daughters when they were first born.

"Don't care for dogs?" Marge asked.

It was the first thing she'd asked Gayle over the
course of the two-hour ride.

"I'm just a bit wary about ones I don't know…"

"Did you ever think about adopting one?"

"No," Gayle replied.

"Why not?" Marge questioned.

Gayle said, "They're an extra expense."

Marge nodded, "Let's run to the supermarket,
grab some groceries for the weekend."

She turned into Whole Foods, cracked the window, and the two of them headed towards the store. Gayle peeked back at the car where Wilbur held his snout at the crack of the window, taking long, slow breaths.

"We should rent a movie," Marge suggested.

They walked to the Redbox. Gayle zoned out as Marge started spouting off movie titles she'd never heard of, movies with 'love' and stupid sounding acronyms in the titles. After six strenuous minutes, Marge decided on a drama about whales and squids, or something along that line. Gayle pulled out her bank card as Marge fumbled through her purse.

"I got it," Gayle said.

"No, no," Marge insisted. "You don't have to do that, I'll ge-"

"I got it, Marge," Gayle swiped her card. "It's the least I can do."

The women went inside, and Marge grabbed a basket. She headed directly for the produce aisle and started skimming vegetables. Gayle glimpsed at a few of the prices and gasped, *Jesus*. She knew there was a reason she didn't shop there. Marge picked up what looked to be salad makings before they made their way to meat aisle.

"Chicken or fish?" Marge looked at Gayle.

Gayle shrugged, "Your choice."

"Brent loves my blackened chicken," Marge said, standing between the poultry and seafood. "He says it's my best dish."

She debated for a while but picked up some cod. They meandered through the section and came across a sample stand where a young man was cutting pieces of filet.

"Be careful," Marge said to him. "That's a great cut of steak."

The twenty-something-year-old shot Marge an I-know-how-to-do-my-job-lady stare, but played it off with a smile.

"Would you ladies like to try," he lifted the platter.

"Delicious," Gayle said after finishing.

"I don't know," Marge chewed her piece excessively slow. "It's a bit over seasoned."

Gayle smiled at the young man, "Well, I like it."

"Hmm," Marge shrugged before looking at the young man's nametag, "Thanks for the bite, Jor... How do you pronounce your name?"

Gayle glanced at Marge, finding it difficult to believe this was the first time she'd seen the name Jorge written down. The young man pronounced his name clearly and slowly in its two syllables as Marge repeated after him.

"Yes, that's right," Jorge said.

"Okay," Marge bellowed in accomplishment. "Where are you from, Jorge?"

Jorge shot Gayle a quick look and Gayle shot him one back.

"Cleveland, ma'am," he said.

"No, I mean your people."

Gayle closed her eyes, she knew she wasn't being punked, she wasn't important enough for that, she was really grocery shopping with this woman. Gayle opened her eyes.

"My grandparents are from Madrid." Jorge asked more than stated.

Marge nodded, "Oh, Spain, explains why the food was over-seasoned. Well, have a nice day, Jorge!"

She laughed as fiercely as she did that day in the class-room, and Gayle was just as silent. They were out of the store in ten minutes, and Marge pulled out her cellphone as they got back into the car.

"My god," Marge blew. "Four missed calls and eleven text messages from the kids. You'd think I'd been gone a week."

Gayle grinned.

"They're completely lost without me," Marge started scrolling through the messages. "Have you heard from yours?"

Gayle shook her head, "Nope. I told them this was mom's weekend, and only to call if it was an emergency."

"Really?" Marge seemed surprised.

"Of course, they can handle themselves," Gayle said.

Marge stopped what she was doing and pocketed her phone. They were on Marge's parents' street shortly after, and every house looked more grandiose than the next. The thought of those mansions being homes-away-from-home for people was as excessive as their stained glass windows, imported cobblestone walkways, and unnaturally green lawns. They pulled into the driveway and Gayle immediately took out her camera. It looked like a house from one of those cheesy acronym love movies, big and beautiful and scenic and maintained; she took three pictures.

"Before I give you the tour, let me put Wilbur in the storage area," Marge said, as she led the dog away.

Gayle watched from a distance as Marge coaxed Wilbur into the home's version of a basement. The space was under the house with an open layout and a screen mesh for walls. Marge locked the doors as she returned to the car.

"Won't he get lonely down here?" Gayle's compassion towards the old dog surprised Marge, but not as much as it did Gayle.

"He'll be with us most of the time, but my parents don't want him inside," Marge explained. "He's used to being down here."

"But won't he get lonely?" Gayle repeated.

Marge didn't respond that time.

"So this is the house," Marge said. "Well, one of them. There's a deck and a couple of hammocks out back by the boat. I'll show you the rest of the place."

Gayle followed Marge and eyed Wilbur as he sat next to the mesh and surveyed the women walk up the stairs. Marge showed Gayle to her room, first—a large two double bedroom with a private bathroom—then she took her to the kitchen, then to the outside patio with a view of the dock and boat, then to the upstairs office and larger patio up there. It was quite the house.

"Well, now that you've seen the place, what do you want to do," Marge asked.

Relax, was what Gayle wanted to say, as the thought of relaxing at a beach house was the only real reason she decided to go along with the farce.

"It's up to you," Gayle said in hopes she could hear the faux tiredness in her voice.

"Let's head back," Marge was pulling out her

keys as she said it.

They returned to the house.

"Go rest on one of the hammocks, I'll get dinner started."

"You sure you don't need any help," Gayle questioned.

"I'm usually cooking for five, so this is a treat," Marge smiled.

Gayle grabbed her camera and mp3 player before heading outside.

"I'll come back in an hour to make the salad, okay," Gayle said.

"Okay," Marge said without turning around.

As Gayle walked out back, she saw Wilbur staring at her from his prison. Had she been a dog person, she might have put his leash on and taken him with her, but she wasn't, so she didn't. She put her music on and knocked out almost instantly, but not before getting a chance to breathe it all in being surrounded by water, sand, and artificially lush grass. She wished her daughters could see it. She wished all three of them had a beach house to escape to instead of mortgage and a two-bedroom bungalow, that her parents could buy her a BMW and she could ditch her '03 Volkswagen, that her ex would stop hiding assets to avoid child support, she wished she had three decks and four hammocks and no job. Gayle took another picture and fell asleep.

She rejoined Marge in the kitchen a while later.

"Smells great in here," Gayle said.

"Thanks," Marge motioned to the counter. "Salad stuff is over there."

Gayle started chopping tomatoes, "This is a gorgeous house, Marge."

"Yeah," Marge nodded. "But the one in Boca is a lot nicer, it has a pool."

Gayle exhaled, "You said your Dad bought this place fifty years ago?"

"Umhmm," Marge continued. "This one and the others. Said he wanted to set things up for my sister and I when he was gone. What a saint?"

Gayle started ripping the lettuce.

"He said he'd make sure we never had anything to worry about," Marge said. "Even when I married Brent, he said, *Anything happens, I'll take care of you, hun.*

"Too bad they can't always take care of us, huh?" Gayle added, "It gets hard at this age, doesn't it? Seeing them starting to need us..."

Marge hesitated for a moment, "Brent's parents are dead, they died in a car accident when we were in college. A year before we got married."

"I'm sorry to hear that," Gayle whispered.

"Dad said we should have waited," Marge started to portion out the rice and fish. "But that's love for you!"

Gayle nodded and laughed.

"I don't know what I'd do without him," Marge chuckled as well, though Gayle wasn't sure which of the two men that had always taken care of her she was referring to.

"I'm done with the salad," Gayle took the bowl over to their plates. "Should we eat outside?"

"Great idea," Marge agreed. "I'll go get Wilbur."

Gayle bit her lip. She hoped he wasn't one of those dogs that would jump all over her for a scrap of food. They sat out on the highest patio and watched the sunset in the distance. It was picturesque — bright orange with hints of pink and soft blues — so picturesque that Gayle put her plate down so she could take a picture for her girls; she didn't even care if Wilbur ate off her plate.

"I thought we'd walk to the beach after dinner, Wilbur could use a bit of time out there," Marge said.

"Sounds good," Gayle replied.

Before they took another bite, the women heard a deafening sound. Marge jumped, Gayle looked around, and Wilbur started to shake. Gayle felt the sound's vibration ricochet off the patio and up her legs into her stomach.

"Christ," Marge put her hand to her chest.

"What was that?" Gayle looked out onto the empty sky as her heartrate quickened.

"I think it was a sonic boom," Marge said. "There's a military base in town."

"That's something breaking the sound barrier, right? A jet?" Gayle asked.

"Yes," Marge replied. "Seems unnatural doesn't it, that something that loud could go un-seen..."

"Like an invisible explosion," Gayle explained.

"Exactly," Marge smiled at Gayle.

Gayle looked down at the still shaking and whimpering Wilbur, "Your dog is scared."

"I know, but I can't coddle him now or he'll think he reacted the right way," Marge put her empty plate down and continued to stare out into the sky, taking long, slow breaths.

Gayle watched Wilbur shake and was com-pelled to offer him a piece of fish, but she didn't, she wasn't a dog person. Gayle took one of her last few bites.

"My husband told me he's leaving," Marge said slowly and clearly, annunciating each sylla-ble. "That he hasn't been happy since before he can remember."

Gayle looked at Marge with a mouthful of fish, "I'm ro rorry-"

Gayle clamped her mouth shut and chewed ferociously, had there been a bone in that fish, she would have choked.

"I'm sorry to hear that, Marge," she corrected herself.

Marge didn't respond, she just stared out into that orange and pink and blue sky, then she grabbed her and Gayle's plates to carry inside. Before going in, she glanced over her shoulder at Gayle.

"Is it hard," Marge whispered. "Doing it alone?"

Gayle wiped her mouth, "Sometimes, but it's not about us, you know?"

"Yeah," Marge nodded. "I guess you're right."

Marge smiled at Gayle before going in. Moments later, Gayle and Wilbur heard another boom. Wilbur started shaking worse than the last time. Gayle stared at him, the dog was terrified of something he didn't, couldn't, understand. She looked into his big wets eyes and listened to his whimpers settle beneath the beats of her heart. Gayle lowered her hand and touched the dog's head, he was so cold. She spread her fingers over his light colored curls.

"Everything's going to be alright," she whispered so lowly so that only he could hear her.

Gayle stroked the dog's head back and forth until he quieted and was no longer shaking, but she continued to comfort him, because she believed she understood, then. She understood why she was there.

THE ATHEIST AND THE ORDINARY

"I'm so tired of this argument," Stace said.

Bernan replied, "I'm not..."

She rolled her eyes at her brother. It always started the same way, every Saturday night Bernan would ask Stace if she was going to church with him and their mother in the morning. Stace would purse her lips, force a strained grin, and kindly decline. Then, Bernan would ask why, and Stace's left eyelid would twitch the way it would when she was about to get pissed, and that's when he knew he had her. That's when it would get started, the same argument they'd been having since they were teenagers.

The two moved in together when Stace got accepted into medical school. She did her undergrad on the other side of the country, and would have preferred to stay there, but as Bernan pointed out, she couldn't pass up a free ride. Moving back into her mother's apartment was out of the question, so she rented a studio downtown. *I'll be closer to the school*, she had told them. Bernan was just a junior at State then.

"Why not get a place together, it'll be cheaper," he suggested.

"You mean you're ready to fly the coop?" Stace laughed.

He didn't bite back in his usual way, he only nodded. So did Stace.

Three years later, she wondered if she made a mistake. Not because she didn't enjoy living with her brother, but because he insisted on carrying on about God every weekend, and even more so on a holiday.

"Damn it, Bernan," Stace snapped. "You're in grad school now, you haven't grown out of this yet?"

Bernan answered with a mouth full of pizza, "You can't grow out of your faith."

"Oh yeah..." Stace grabbed a slice. "What about Ali?"

"He didn't grow out of it," Bernan explained. "He just found a new one."

"Doesn't that mean he grew out of the old

one?" Stace asked.

Bernan shook his head, "Religions might differ, but faith is faith."

Shit, Stace almost said.

"What about me," Stace questioned. "I grew out of mine…"

"You have to have something in order to grow out of it."

"I did —" Stace stopped herself.

Bernan looked up from his pizza, "So what happened?"

Shit.

Bernan had been fishing around that pond for over a decade, ever since Stace decreed that the Easter Vigil of '03 would be her last church service.

"Why," he asked her.

"Because I'm not playing anymore," she said.

Bernan was a mature eleven-year-old, but he didn't understand, "Playing what?"

"Pretend," was all she said.

When Bernan got older, he tried to figure out why she no longer said her prayers with him, why she'd roll her eyes every time their mother kissed the rosary hanging in the kitchen, why everyone that believed was a nearsighted sheep, and she a farsighted wolf.

"You know being nearsighted means you see what's directly in front of you," he said to her once while in college.

"It also means everything else is a blur," she replied.

"So are things close by, when you're farsighted," Bernan said.

"I'd rather be able to see into the distance," Stace said.

"Well, I'd rather be able to see what's right in front of me."

"You mean what's been put in front of you?" she asked.

"I mean, what's right in front of me," he replied.

"Just drop it," Stace said.

"Fine," Bernan hesitated. "Mom asked for you, today."

Stace let out an exasperated exhale loud enough to wake the landlord two floors down, "What the hell, man. Can I just eat my dinner?"

"She wants you to call her," Bernan continued. "You should..."

"Don't tell me what I should do," Stace said.

"Are you seriously still mad," Bernan

crossed his arms. "If I've forgiv—"

"Don't," Stace interrupted.

"What," Bernan shrugged. "You won't talk to me about Mom, about going to church on Easte—"

"Fuck, Bernan," Stace threw her crust at his head. "Enough!"

Bernan picked up the crust that hit his temple and tossed it in the pizza box before he took a long look at his older sister.

"I know you stopped believing, Stacy," Bernan whispered. "But when did you get so angry about it?"

Bernan's dark eyes penetrated hers, she wanted to look away, but knew he'd win if she did.

"I'm not angry, Bernan," Stace said. "I'm just so tired of this argument."

"Come to bed, Lishio," Mrs. Melino shouted down from the top of the stairs.

She'd started calling him that name shortly after they left Italy. He shared his first name with his father, and couldn't bear to hear it every day. On the plane ride, Mr. Melino asked his then new wife to use his middle name as they fled. She did. They watched from the sky as the hillsides, crosses, cobblestone, and vineyards they'd known morphed into specks of memory that would soon be more reminiscent of a dream than their home. They were nineteen and in love, and ashamed. It seemed so long ago.

"Va beh," Mr. Melino replied. "Soon."

He stood in his makeshift wine cellar, cleaning the six bottles he first corked when they moved into the house thirty-five years ago. The cloth he used was soft and delicate, the same way he was with the bottles. Mr. Melino wiped the necks, gently brushing decades of dust away. He made sure the bottles were immaculate before he wrapped and put them in his wicker basket, not a fleck or finger-print; tomorrow wasn't about how well-aged the wine was, it wasn't about Mr. Melino either, it was about his son.

The wine cellar was actually the laundry room, a small basement only big enough for the furnace, but stuffed to the letter with a washer dryer set, holiday ornaments, wine racks, and the wooden basins his grapes would ferment in. Mrs. Melino desperately wanted the bulky racks out of there, as they made it impossible for two people to be in the basement at once, but they were all her husband had left of his father — those wine racks and his grapes.

When they bought their home, it wasn't the cost, neighborhood, or fixtures that sold them, it was the massive grapevine covering the awning on the back patio. *The vine is healthy and strong*, the realtor had said. *If cared for correctly, it will outlive the two of you.* Mr. Melino already knew that. His father owned a small vineyard back home, and Mr. Melino and his brother were practically raised with the grapes. The boys would pick, eat, clean, eat, squash, sip, and bottle daily; they aged with the wine they produced, and a young Mr. Melino felt it just as much his investment as his father's.

He still remembered how it felt, to submerge his hands deep within a barrel of grapes, watching them disappear amongst the deep violets and sometimes greens, but mostly violets. The tartness that would seep into his nostrils, the way it would make him wince in the best way. What Mr. Melino remembered most was pulling his arms out of the grapes, the cool slither they'd exit with, taking some of the grape skin with him and leaving some of his skin behind, bits of himself stuck in the process, knowing that whoever tasted their wine would be tasting him too. He remembered how his arms would be stained red for the rest of the day, how he never tried to wash it away, how it was the first time he felt he was really a part of something.

While Mr. Melino's father was a vintner, his first love was the church. That love was passed down to his children, and propelled Mr. Melino's father to see to it that his eldest boy joined the priesthood. His father invested almost as much of his energy into both his grapes and his son, becoming a priest. *There's no greater gift, mio figlio, then serving one's father*, his father would say to him. Too many times to count.

Mr. Melino quietly trudged upstairs after taking another half an hour to properly pack his basket. He'd have to leave early the next morning to deliver the wine before mass, as it was no typical Easter Vigil. This Sunday would be first of nine that his only son would be acting as the church's diocesan administrator, its temporary ordinary. Mr. Melino knew it was just a formality, he knew his son would receive the permanent position. He considered it the church's informal probationary period, seeing how the forty-five-year-old priest would handle his post.

Mr. Melino crept into the bedroom, the lights were off and he could hear Mrs. Melino's faint but recognizable snore, even though she affirmed that she did no such thing. He pulled off his stained t-shirt and jeans, he was too tired to shower. Before crawling into bed, Mr. Melino caught a shaded look at his reflection, the moon his only light. He turned to his side and back to the front.

"*Sono vecchio,*" he mumbled under his breath, *he looked so old.*

He was only sixty-five, but felt he looked eighty. It was the job that aged him, laying concrete for forty years will do that.

"No," Mrs. Melino whispered. "Not so old."

She smiled at him, he smiled back.

"*Scusate, Bellezza,*" Mr. Melino apologized as he got into bed. "I didn't want wake you."

It almost scared him as to how little she had aged. Not a grey hair intertwined in those loose brown ringlets, and just a few lines around her smile. Her eyes were still as big and as full as the first time he saw her. She nuzzled onto his chest and he wrapped his arm around her.

"He will do good tomorrow, Lishio," Mrs. Melino whispered. "Takes after Papa."

Mr. Melino knew where this was going.

"You would have been good, too…" Mrs. Melino glanced up at him.

"*Bellezza,*" Mr. Melino shook his head. "*Per favore…*"

"I just sayin'," she went on.

"No," he interrupted.

He pulled his arm away and shifted his body towards his side of the bed. Mrs. Melino tried to readjust with him, but it was impossible, he had moved too far away.

"I just a man, *mi amore*," he kissed her cheek and rolled to his side.

Mrs. Melino thought about the nights when he would spend too many hours preparing his wine for mass, instead of sleeping; or when they had guests and he would talk about their son, his father's vineyard, and the first time he saw the inside of St. Mark's Basilica; how wondrous all of those things were. Mrs. Melino wanted to understand why, why her husband thought being *just a man*, wasn't enough.

Stace barely got a wink of sleep. She was used to her brother's prying but wasn't used to not being able to keep her composure. The only people that could upset her were the two she lived with the longest; Bernan and her mother. Bernan would just push sometimes, like he did the night before, and make Stace regret that anyone had that sort of power over her.

Her mother on the other hand, was an astute passivist, and a drunk. Once when Stace attempted to address her drinking, her mother dismissed her as she sipped the third can of Coors Light with her eggs and bacon. The only time Stace's mother was sober was at church. She'd wake up with the Saturday night hangover, drink six cups of coffee, and get it together for nine o'clock Mass. Looking at the three of them, no one would have any idea. Bernan would spend most of Mass glued to her hip, and their mother would coddle him, let him snuggle up to her the way she should have when they were at home, but she preferred the company of wine. That was her beverage of choice, she'd drink anything, but would choose red wine over everything. Stace believed her mother found a refinement in wine, a sort of class that didn't exist with other liquors. She supposed the rest of the world saw it that way too, that's why it was wine *tasting,* unlike *chugging, guzzling,* or *downing.*

Unlike her brother, Stace would sit two rows behind them at mass, absolutely furious that her mother could find it in herself to sober up for the Lord, and not for her children. She would sometimes imagine her mother losing control when they'd go up for communion. She'd imagine her sipping the wine — they did not use grape juice at that church — and being overcome with the same irresistible urge she was overcome with whenever she stepped in the house. She'd imagine her mother snatching the chalice out of the priest's hands, finishing the offering with a single swig, then pushing the priest out of the way and dunking her head deep down into the wine basin, swallowing mouthfuls. Stace imagined it as she'd lean against the pew waiting for her mother and brother to take communion; it never did happen.

Stace needed to get out of the apartment, she didn't want to be around Bernan when he was getting dressed. He'd try to do something inadvertent, ask her to help him with his tie or something, all so he could start pushing again. She grabbed a few medical texts and poured herself a cup of oolong before getting in the car. It was a bit foggy. She wanted to be someplace quiet, the university quad, where she could sip her tea, glance through her texts, and free her mind of the day having anything to do with a resurrection.

Stace and Bernan moved to the little residential area a year earlier, cheaper rent and more space. Most mornings, before the sun and everyone else awoke, she found solitude in the empty neighborhood. She embraced every bumpy back road and uneven pot hole, and would relish in resting her bare left foot outside the open window; in going over twenty in a school zone, in usually forgetting to turn her headlights on, and in gliding through red lights and not coming to a complete stop at stop signs; she embraced the fact that even an atheist could sometimes feel like a god.

Stace heard her phone ping and immediately knew it was one of them. Only her mother or Ber-

nan would have the audacity to text her at 6:37am!
She opened the message; it was from her mother:

Happy Easter, Stacy, Bernan said you weren't coming... Change your mind, girl... I'm getting back in AA Tues and want to see you.

Her mother started going to Alcoholics Anonymous three times in the past seven years. When she first tried to get clean, Stace wasn't sure who she was angrier at. Her mother, for deciding to get clean after her children were grown, Bernan, for forgiving her, or herself, for wanting to forgive her too. She said she was sober for about four months before she relapsed, but Stace was sure it was sooner.

Stace approached an intersection as she finished reading her mother's message: *Service starts at 9, but you gotta be there early to get a good seat. We'll save you one, don't be late. God bless you, Stacy.* Stace gripped the wheel. She said the words over and over as her foot tensed on the gas. When she told her mother that she had stopped believing in God, her mother said, *God bless you, Stacy.* When Stace thanked her, but said that she didn't want the blessing, her mother said it again, *God bless you, Stacy.* When Stace explained that she wouldn't impose her views on her, so she shouldn't either, her mother repeated, *God bless you, Stacy.* When

Stace came right out and asked her to please stop using the phrase, her mother smiled and said it anyway, *God bless you, Stacy.*

It had stopped being about the words for both of them so long ago. Stace hated how damn vindictive her mother could be, that she considered herself a faith-driven woman. That she'd recite scripture while in a drunken stoop as Stace and Bernan dragged her into bed.

"You've got to forgive people, Stacy," her mother once pleaded.

"I'm not a Christian anymore, remember?" Stace replied. "So, no, I don't."

Stace glared at her phone as the traffic light turned yellow, it almost looked green, mixed into the hazy blue hue of morning. She read the four words with her temper flaring, Stace shook her head, "God bless my a —."

Mr. Melino snuck out of bed before sunrise, he wanted to get an early start, a habit he picked up when he first joined the church. He began his religious studies at the age of eight, splitting his time between the church and the vineyard. He soon grew as invested in the holy book as he had his father's grapes. He was appointed head altar server when he was ten. Young Mr. Melino reveled in dressing in his robes every Sunday, in laying them out the night before, in gliding down the side of the aisle so soundly the flame of his candle barely shook, in arranging the pall and chalice before service, in watching the reactions of the patrons as he did it, their appreciation, their love.

Mr. Melino continued up the Catholic Church ranks and had made up his mind when he was seventeen that he was going to be a priest. When he told his father, the man stood in front of him and started to cry. Mr. Melino had never seen him cry. His father wrapped his arms around him, held him tight, and Mr. Melino felt his father's tears trickle off of his cheek and onto his own forehead. The tears were dewy, and warm. Mr. Melino did not wipe them away, he just held his father as his father held him, and on that day Mr. Melino understood what it meant for someone to be proud. And that was why he could never face him again, why Mr. Melino chose to leave the church, grapes, and family he loved so much, and those warm, dewy tears.

Mr. Melino retrieved the basket of wine bottles he readied the previous night and sat it in his metal-caged cart. He preferred walking the wine to church before mass, it was only a few blocks away and he enjoyed the serenity of morning; the world was always so quiet in the morning. He kissed a sleeping Mrs. Melino's forehead before he left, he always did.

Mr. Melino strolled outside, pushing his cart and the oldest bottles he had in the cellar. He walked on the side of the street to avoid sidewalk edges when he transported wine, it led for a smoother journey. It was too special an occasion for any of his other bottles, he needed the best today, his son needed the best. Mr. Melino knew his son was destined for the priesthood, he saw it in the boy's passion for the Word, but mostly, in his faith. Mr. Melino thought he himself was committed, but understood after watching his son, that was not so.

Years earlier, Mr. Melino watched his son stop in the middle of the street and intertwine his fingers with a homeless man wearing a rosary. He watched as they bowed their heads and people stared at the two—the man in his twenty layers of clothing in the midst of July's heat and the boy with his head pressed against his.

Mr. Melino smiled at his son later, "You are saint."

His son took his hand, "Maybe one day..."

"No," Mr. Melino assured. "This day."

Mr. Melino rolled his cart across the street as he pictured seeing his son that morning, fully ordained in the community he'd served his entire life. The next step was bishop, Mr. Melino knew, his son had already spent time at the Vatican and met with two Popes. The highest post Mr. Melino made it up to in the church was that of a diaconate, and then he left for the West. It was times like these he wished his own father still alive, to show him that everything wasn't in vain, he did indeed produce a priest.

Mr. Melino noticed the latch on his cart was unhooked. He tried to close it, but it appeared to be broken. Mr. Melino took extra careful steps as he continued down the street. The last time he walked so meticulously was as he first entered St. Mark's Basilica. The church might as well have been a monument; it towered above all else and sparkled with a gold tinge under the light of the sun. Every detail, archway, curve, and twist in its design was immaculate. As he stepped into the church, he lost his breath, he'd been struck in the gut.

Mr. Melino gazed into the bluish haze of the morning as he crossed at an intersection. His thoughts were countries away, nestled in the church that changed his life forever. He was more than half-way across the road when he was overcome with a warmth, the same warmth he felt when his father hugged him, when he saw his son and the old man, and when he first stepped into St. Mark's and saw —

Stace felt the impact before the sound resonated and she saw him. A heavy blast ricocheting off the hood of her car then onto her windshield, and what sounded like a million shards of glass imploding onto the street.

"Oh my god," Stace shouted as she slammed on brakes.

The man tumbled off the side of her car, rolling onto the street. Stace jumped out of the vehicle and went around the front of the car when she saw the old man lying on his back.

"Shit," Stace ran towards him.

She called 911 seconds later, and was told they had been dispatched to her location.

The operator asked, "Is he responsive?"

Stace got on her knees and said, "Can you hear me, sir?"

The man's eyes shifted to hers, but he didn't respond.

"Yes, please hurry!" Stace set the phone down beside her.

Stace examined him, surprisingly, no blood save a busted lip and a few scratches.

"Okay, sir," she leaned in. "I'm going to unbutton your shirt and check for bruising. I'm a doctor."

It wasn't a complete lie; she was *almost* a doctor. He looked at her again as Stace calmly undressed him. He was old, in his seventies maybe. His hair was more whitish than gray and his skin a burnt leathery bronze.

"Can you speak?" Stace asked.

"Ye—," the man started to cough and Stace saw what she believed were small specks of blood landing on his lip.

She hurried with the rest of his shirt and wanted to gasp, but kept her composure. The bruising on his abdomen was consistent with a punctured lung. She could see the broken ribs underneath his skin, their red-violet tinge stood out like a stained glass portrait on his torso. The man continued to cough and Stace could hear the blood in his throat, he was sweating profusely. She tried to sit him up, but his pain was too intense. She felt her calmness begin to waver as she knew the issue was on the inside, and she couldn't do anything about it.

That's when she saw it, the decorated gold cross that had fallen to the side of the man's neck.

"I'm so sorry," Stace's voice shook. "I didn't see you."

The man continued to cough and began to wheeze. She thought of her brother then, and the gold cross around his neck. Had this been Bernan lying in the street, she knew what he'd want someone to do.

Stace took hold of the man's hand and began, "Our Father, who art in heaven, hallowed be thy name..."

The man's eyes began to close. Stace continued reciting the Lord's Prayer, but found her nervousness heightened.

"Thy kingdom come, thy will be done, on earth as it is in heaven," she started speaking immensely slow.

Her nerves weren't only on edge because of the dying man who lay below her, the dying man that she was responsible for, but because she hadn't thought about the prayer in so long, because she didn't remember how it ended.

"Give us this day, our daily bread..."

Mr. Melino listened to the young woman praying over him.

He wanted to join her in reciting the prayer, but he was out of breath and every time he tried to speak, he tasted blood, and would cough. The taste reminded him of a spoiled batch of grapes he picked once, soured and shiny.

"And forgive us our trespasses," the woman whispered as she squeezed his hand, he wanted to squeeze back, but couldn't.

Everything became a blur then, the woman above him, and the world around him. Everything went dark. In the darkness, Mr. Melino was able to muster the memory he was about to recall before he felt the cold steel of the vehicle hammer into his side.

Mr. Melino didn't think of his son, or his father, or his grapes and vines, he didn't think of robes or chalices or of the time a woman yelled he was more olive than white, and he didn't even think of St. Mark's, he thought of the thing that was inside.

Only months before he was set to formally join the church, Mr. Melino saw a young nun standing near the pew hidden amongst the rest of her sisters. He saw her eyes before he saw anything else, they were so big and so full, they were the type of eyes that made everything else seem so small. He gazed into them the same way he would when he'd sneak to her window at the abbey, when he told her he loved her, when she said she did too, when that love grew too intense to control, too strong against their vows, when she told him that she was expecting their child, when he told her they had to leave and start a new life, that they couldn't put their families through the looming storm, when she told him she would go anywhere with him, when he told her how guilty he felt about making her choose, when she assured him she would have done it all over again, when he tried to call his father once in the new country, but his father didn't take the call, and then he cried in her arms and felt tears roll from his cheeks and onto her forehead, the tears she didn't wipe away.

"As we forgive them that trespass against us," he heard the woman kneeling above him almost sing.

Mr. Melino's mouth filled with blood as the image of his wife faded. The last thing he would see, his Bellezza, the only thing in his life that made being *just a man*, more than enough.

Stace felt the man's hand go limp and she froze in a panic. The man took his final breath as she recited the last line she could remember of the prayer. She was still, huddled over him in the middle of the intersection. Stace heard the sirens in the distance, but stayed on her knees, her hands still wrapped around the man's. It was the same position she took when she used to pray, not with Bernan, when she'd pray on her own.

Stace could see the flashing lights in her peripheral and remembered the flashes she'd see as a child. Her mother, wailing on Bernan, beating him like a toy, a broken doll. Pounding him senselessly because he reminded her of their father, of the man that beat her senseless and forced her into numbing her pain with a bottle of wine; flashes Stace hated looking directly at because she knew she couldn't stop her, because when her mother would catch her staring she'd look her dead in the eyes as she lifted her belt, and Stace would shake on the inside, but she would never look away. She knew her mother would win if she looked away.

She let go of the old man's hand and lifted her eyes from his closed and quiet ones. She didn't see the cops pull up, or the paramedics running towards them. She couldn't see anything right in front of her. The only thing Stace saw was the old man's turned-over cart, laying crooked in the street, and all the red wine seeping out of his basket. She watched the wine glide down the side of the road so soundly, escaping the exploded glass and tattered twine decorating the once barren street. But when she looked closer, the wine didn't appear to moving away from the shards and threads at all, it almost looked as though it was headed towards something. She was sure of it then, the wine looked as though it was headed for something, more.

Stone Fishing

Willy was spending half the summer with his grandparents. Not the ones with the well-lit condo, the ones with a 95-year-old wheat farm; not the ones with an eight-foot pool out back, the ones with a rusted tractor and beat up red shed. He wouldn't have gone had he been given a choice, but ten-year-olds aren't given many of those.

Grandma, a plump liver-spotted woman, knitted. She'd knit scarves, hats, dishcloths, socks, ponchos, coasters, armbands, headbands, and anything else. Grandpa, a thin sun-bleached man, spent his time doing crosswords—sometimes a book a day. They took up their hobbies a year or so after Willy was born, when they realized they could no longer manage the wheat.

Besides knitting and crosswords, Grandma would cook three squares a day—Willy had never eaten so much in his life — and Grandpa would take care of the dog he adopted some years back. "He comes and goes," Grandpa told Willy. "Don't see Dog two, three days sometimes. But he always comes back." Grandpa never named the dog; just called him Dog. He'd put fresh water out for him every hour and he'd keep him clean, utterly tick free. On his fourth day there, Willy saw Grandpa get a firm grip of one of the little suckers. The tick had latched on under Dog's neck and had been feasting.

"See how fat he is," Grandpa said. "Means he's been eatin' for days."

"Eating what?" Willy asked.

"Blood," Grandpa answered.

"So it's like a vampire?"

"No." Grandpa spoke firmly. "It's like a tick."

Grandpa twisted and pulled on the insect, struggling to remove it from the otherwise clean animal, and Willy cringed when Dog cowered in an awful sort of pain. "There," Grandpa said. "Got him." Willy watched as Grandpa laid the bug on the stone porch step and grabbed hold of the banister.

"Stop that," Grandma shouted from the window. "That's not something for a boy his age to see." Grandpa did not stop. Willy watched as the thin old man pointed his toe to the clouds and slowly lowered the heel of his heavy workman's boot into the tick. Dog's blood squirted from the insect's behind. This also made Willy cringe, but it had admittedly been the most entertaining thing he'd seen in days.

His grandparents didn't own the technologies that usually kept Willy occupied. They had no computer and therefore no internet. They had no TV, thus, no game system. They didn't even have any good books, just the ones that used to belong to Willy's mother. *Moby what?* Willy wrinkled his nose. "Gross!" They had everything they needed and always found something to do.

A week had passed. Willy was lying on the living room floor watching the ceiling fan, and the sound of Grandma's clickity clacking needles paired with Grandpa's pencil noises were driving him up the wall. But as Willy could not climb walls, he complained.

"There's nothing to do," said Willy. "I'm bored."

Grandpa said, "You kids today need to learn how to entertain yourselves."

Willy coyly rolled his eyes.

"Why not go outside for a while, dear," Grandma suggested.

Anywhere would be better than where he was, so he went.

"It even smells boring out here," he mumbled as the smell of raw wheat and dirt twisted into his nostrils.

Willy looked out onto the wheat field and tilted his head in the direction the stalks were leaning; it was a windy day. He shoved his hands into his pockets and began to drag his feet across the driveway dirt that had settled around his grandfather's car. It was fun, at first, until a cloud of dirt picked up and surrounded Willy. The cloud was overbearing, intrusive even. Willy coughed. He ran from the cloud and walked around back, brushing the dirt from his camo orange shorts. Then, something caught Willy's attention.

There was a long narrow divot bordering the wheat field, but instead of sand, the space was filled with piles of rocks. Small ones, big ones, gray ones, brown ones, and some the size of baseballs. He reached into the divot and picked up one of the smaller stones. Willy was squeezing the rock and glancing out upon the miles of dusted beige when he was overcome by an overwhelming sensation, an urge that sent tingles down his fingers, and an uncontrollable jolt up his arm and into his shoulder. Willy wanted to throw that rock, hard and far, with authority, perhaps even with purpose. Willy pulled his arm back, launching the stone so vigorously he nearly threw his shoulder out. The rock soared higher than anything Willy had ever thrown and landed somewhere in the rows of wheat. Willy grabbed hold of his shoulder, only noticing the pain once the stone had settled, and grinned a wide sort of sideways grin.

"I want to do that again!"

And so he did. He chose a big one next. Willy spun around in the rocky divot, swinging the large stone with his momentum, and let it go off into the field. He listened as the large stone landed with a thud and it seemed to traipse between the wheat stocks. The sideways smile didn't get a chance to return before Willy heard someone trudging up from behind, their footsteps emulating the thudding sound he'd recently admired.

"Hey, boy," Grandpa yelled. "What the hell are you doing?"

No one had ever cursed at Willy, until then.

"Throwing rocks," he answered quietly.

"What for?"

Willy shrugged.

"Well, stop it now," Grandpa snapped, pulling Willy out of the divot. "Don't you know idle hands are the devil's workshop?"

Willy shook his head.

"They are, and throwing rocks for no good reason is idle. Find something useful to do."

"Like what?" Willy asked.

Grandpa paused. "Not this… it's dangerous. Don't be throwing anymore rocks, Willy. You understand me?"

Willy nodded but wasn't sure if Grandpa meant throwing rocks was dangerous, or idle hands were. Grandpa went back in the house—to finish a crossword no doubt—and Willy followed. Grandma called him to the kitchen a minute later. She needed help preparing supper. She handed him a bowl of green beans that needed the ends snapped and a couple of corncobs that needed to be shucked. Willy made sure to sit in a seat facing the back window. That way he could still keep an eye on the divot. It's not that Willy thought it was going to run away or anything, or that he was planning on disobeying Grandpa, he just wanted to look at it. Grandma stopped cooking momentarily and found a small piece of paper. She jotted a few things down and headed into the living room.

Grandpa stuck his head into the kitchen. "You want to run to the grocery store, Willy?"

Before he had a chance to respond, Grandma did. "He's snapping beans right now."

Grandpa fumbled around, and then Willy

heard the car engine revving up and pulling out of the driveway. He finished with the beans and corn a few minutes later.

"Thank you, Willy." Grandma gently tapped his shoulder. "You run along now."

In less than a minute, Willy ended up out back by the stone divot near the wheat field with a rock in his hand. He didn't remember moseying onto the porch, glancing down the road to see if a particular off-white vehicle was returning home, nearly tripping over Dog as he napped on the porch step, tiptoeing past the kitchen window as to not distract Grandma from her cooking, or even bending down and grabbing the stone he held. He didn't remember any of that, though that must have been what he did.

Willy rubbed the rock between his fingers, tracing the rock's surface with his thumb; it was grainy and dense. It wasn't right, having his only pastime taken away like that. Willy turned around, his eyes darting from the driveway to the kitchen window and back to the driveway. He shifted the rock from his palm to his fingertips. It wasn't fair for Grandpa to get mad at him that way. He squeezed. They were just a few little stones. Tighter. No one would miss them...

Another week passed, and Willy could have sworn

his throwing arm had gotten stronger. Willy had stopped seeing the fun in anything besides those stones; he'd sit around most of the day, waiting for Grandpa to leave so he could go throw them. When he couldn't throw any, he busied the time twiddling his thumbs, imagining himself throwing them. He'd mumble under his breath whenever he was told to do a chore or sigh if he was asked to do much of anything at all.

Willy was helping Grandma make lunch when Grandpa came into the kitchen.

"Get that dirty bowl out of here," Grandma shrieked. "We're cooking!"

"I'll just be minute, need some cool water is all," Grandpa said turning on the faucet.

"That Dog's on one of his mating stints anyway; isn't even here," Grandma snarled.

"Should still set some water out though." Grandpa filled the bowl.

"It's a waste of time." Grandma gave Grandpa a look.

"No, it's not," Willy interrupted. "Grandpa's just making sure he doesn't have idle hands."

Grandpa smiled the same smile Willy would see cross his mother's face when something made her happy.

"That's right, boy." Grandpa rubbed his head. "That's right!"

Grandpa took the bowl outside, then called Willy to the front porch.

"Get your shoes on," Grandpa told him. "We're going into town."

Willy stuck his feet into his sneakers and reluctantly tied his shoes; Grandpa was already in the car. Willy's walk was labored as he made his way to the vehicle. *This is supposed to be rock throwing time*, he thought. He yanked at the rusty handle and flopped down into the passenger seat.

The car ride into town was quiet, but Grandpa was a quiet man. The radio was on so low Willy could barely hear it.

"Could you turn the radio up, Grandpa?"

He shook his head, "No, Willy—I like to do some thinking when I drive."

"What do you think about?"

"Oh," Grandpa shifted his hands on the steering wheel, "different things."

"Like what?"

He paused. "I think about you and your mama a lot."

"What about us?"

"How far away you live, how little I get to see you..." Grandpa looked at Willy.

Willy echoed, "What else?"

"Anything that comes to mind, I guess," he answered.

Grandpa thought about telling Willy some of the things that often crossed his mind on his way to town. About his father who worked two jobs and still managed to tend the land he passed down to him, about his mother who loved collecting trinkets because she couldn't afford them as a child, about the brother he lost during the second World War, about the little sister that used to look just like him, about his favorite uncle who disappeared 62 years ago, about the first woman he married that left him for an old boyfriend, about how that drove him to the bottle, about the woman he met after returning from Vietnam he was sure he could never love as much as his first wife but was proven wrong when he looked into her eyes and softened a way he never knew he could — the same way he softened every morning they woke up together for fifty years, the same way he softens when he watches her knit and she nags him about bringing a dirty dog bowl into the kitchen — about how he gave up the bottle after he dropped Willy's mother at two weeks old, about why it hurt him so much when his only daughter moved away to live with his soon-to-be son-in-law, or about how much Willy reminded him of his younger self. He thought about telling Willy some of those things, but they had already arrived in town.

They pulled up to a small antique shop and stepped a few steps from car door to store door. The shop had a weird smell, like Old Spice and something sweet.

"I'm looking for an anniversary gift," Grandpa said. "A couple weeks after you leave, your Grandma and I will be celebrating our 51st."

"Fifty-first what?" Willy asked.

"Wedding anniversary, boy," Grandpa stated. "Let's look around a bit, see if we can find something."

They walked the aisles, and Willy could still smell what might be oranges. He followed closely behind Grandpa, only stopping when the old man paused to examine a jewelry set or music box, and then a painting that hung on the wall closest them caught Willy's attention. Willy approached the painting and admired the pastoral setting accented with green and yellow hues under strokes of sky blue so vivid he thought it might have been a photograph.

He stepped closer, that scent of oranges tickling his nose. There was a shoeless boy leaning against a massive tree — Willy wasn't sure what kind of tree — with a fishing rod in hand and beige hat covering his eyes. Willy took another step. The boy was sitting on an elevated riverbank, at least fifteen feet higher than the water, unable to see the river beneath him. The smell was getting stronger. Willy scanned the painting, his nose some inches away, when he realized that the boy's lure was not actually in the water. It was stuck between two oddly shaped stones parallel to the riverbed, and the boy was none the wiser.

"Ha!" Willy chortled louder than he meant to.

"Keep it down," Grandpa whispered as he joined Willy before pulling him away from the painting. "What's so funny?"

"That picture." Willy pointed, still giggling. "The boy is fishing for stones."

Grandpa looked at the painting, and back at Willy. "That's not funny, it's stupid."

Grandpa walked back to the necklace he'd been examining.

"How's it stupid?" Willy mumbled.

"He's just sitting there, wasting time," Grandpa explained.

"He's not just sitting there. He's fishing," Willy responded.

"For stones, remember…" Grandpa glanced at Willy.

"It's not wasting time if he's having fun," Willy

said with mild authority.

Grandpa said, "Do you think it'd be fun to sit by a riverbed all day and not catch a single fish?"

Willy shrugged. "I dunno..."

Grandpa let out a bit of chuckle. "It's pointless, like you wasted the whole damn day."

Willy's attention was drawn from the painting and onto his grandfather. Willy had never noticed how tall he was or the slight raspy texture to his voice, how his words emanated a type of wisdom; how everything about his grandfather was commanding and tender at the same time.

Grandpa wrapped his long fingers around Willy's shoulder. "That boy fishing for stones is doing a whole lot of nothing. When you start doing nothing you get comfortable doing nothing, then you don't want to do anything but nothing, and sooner or later you realize that's all you've done. Understand?"

Willy nodded.

Grandpa said, "Now let's buy this necklace."

The two were walking to the front when Willy asked, "What's that smell, Grandpa?"

Grandpa dug into his pocket and gave Willy a five dollar bill. "Why don't you go next door and see."

Willy took the money and ran before Grandpa

had a chance to change his mind; no one had ever let him go into a store by himself before. When Willy got outside he saw where the smell was coming from and was surprised he had missed it before. There was a woman selling freshly squeezed orange juice in a cart next to the antique shop. Willy bought two cups. Grandpa was waiting by the car when Willy got back.

"Is that for me?" Grandpa asked extending his hand.

Willy nodded. "You have some change too."

"Keep it," Grandpa said, winking.

The two sipped their orange juice on the ride home. The juice was a bit sour; Willy didn't finish the cup. When they pulled up to the house, Grandpa didn't turn the car off.

"Tell your grandmother I'll be back by supper."

Grandpa took off and Willy started for the house. If the orange juice had been sweeter, Willy would have run inside to let Grandma take a sip. Instead, he sat on the porch and put the cup on the same step Grandpa laid the tick on. Grandpa's wheel dust had settled, and Willy felt the urge coming on. He knew he shouldn't, especially after Grandpa bought him an orange juice. He knew he shouldn't.

Willy stood up and shoved his hands in pockets, the dollar bills Grandpa gave him scratching his knuckles. He inched towards the side of the house, just far enough to see the divot. He knew he shouldn't. His fingers tingled and that familiar jolt seized up in his arm. Willy looked at the sour juice he should go throw away, and then he looked at the divot. The painting's humor was not yet out of Willy's mind.

"Just one," Willy uttered. "I'll just throw one today."

Willy's last week was upon him and so was the secret. The thrill he found in those rocks had steadily flourished on the edge of the wheat field. His throws had grown more forceful, snapping pieces of wheat clean off their stalks.

At the breakfast table one morning, Grandpa started the chatter.

"Haven't seen Dog in a while, have you?" he asked Grandma.

"Come to think if it," she replied, "no. Not for a week or so."

"Odd," Grandpa uttered. "What about you, Willy?"

Willy shook his head. "Nope."

Grandpa put his fork down, dabbed his mouth, and took a gulp of his lukewarm coffee.

"Better go look around." He stood. "See if I can

find him."

It didn't feel like a whole day, but Grandpa didn't return until sunset.

"Nothing?" Grandma probed.

Grandpa flopped down beside her. "No. I'll go out again tomorrow."

Grandma stopped knitting and forced a smile. She pursed her lips and looked at Grandpa like she had something to say, but instead kissed his cheek and squeezed his hand.

Willy, lying on the floor, spun onto his side and watched the beads of sweats fall down Grandpa's forehead.

"I'll go with you tomorrow, Grandpa," Willy said. "I'll help you look for Dog."

"Thank you, Willy," Grandpa said nodding.

They ate, slept, woke, and ate again before Grandpa and Willy set out in search of Dog. They drove all the way to the stoplight closest to town before Grandpa changed directions.

"Let's see if any neighbors have seen him," Grandpa suggested.

They stopped by almost every house between town and home. The inquiries about Dog quickly transformed into introductions to Willy, but no one had seen him. The visits took longer than expected. When Grandpa pulled up to the house, Grandma was waiting on the porch.

"What took so long?" she huffed. "The boy hasn't eaten since breakfast."

"I'm not hungry, Grandma," Willy lied. "We had some snacks."

"Snacks aren't a meal, Willy." Grandma said. "Come, let's make you a sandwich before dinner."

Willy expected Grandpa to follow them, but he didn't. Grandpa looked out onto the rows of wheat, and before Willy got inside, he saw Grandpa's long legs striding towards the field. It seemed to get dark quicker that night, glittered stars imposed on the great blackness surrounding Willy and Grandma in the house. Grandpa still hadn't returned. Grandma would peek outside when she thought Willy wasn't looking, but he saw her do it every time. He was worried too. Willy's bedtime rolled around and Grandma tucked him in.

Willy couldn't sleep. He lay awake for an hour before he heard the jangling of keys and Grandma's pitter-pattering towards the front door.

"Where've you been?" She whisper-yelled. "Worrying me to death."

Grandpa didn't respond. Willy heard Grandma's muffled voice through the wall and gradually let it rock him to sleep, but he was awoken, not two hours later.

"Huh?" Willy grunted.

"Keep it down," Grandpa snapped. "You'll wake your grandma."

Grandpa was holding Willy's shoes and jacket.

"Get dressed," Grandpa said. "We're going for a walk."

Willy couldn't understand where Grandpa would be taking him in the middle of the night or why they'd be going somewhere when Grandma was asleep, but he followed him. Grandpa stopped by the shed and grabbed a camping flashlight. He still hadn't told Willy where they were going, but Willy could see they were heading directly into the wheat field.

It was windy out that night—the wheat stocks leaned as they did before—and Grandpa headed through them motioning for Willy to keep up. He was walking so quickly that Willy was practically running behind him. The wheat was about as tall as Grandpa; Willy couldn't remember a time he'd felt so small. Stalks of blowing wheat struck Willy atop the head as the wind howled a deadened moan that spooked him. The soft ground melded around his feet, keeping him off-balance as he continued behind Grandpa. They hadn't walked too far into the field when Grandpa stopped. He faced Willy, a stern air embedded in his expression, and pointed the flashlight directly beside his feet.

"Do you know what that is," Grandpa asked.

Willy exhaled, finally understanding why Grandpa pulled him out of bed. "A rock..."

He held his breath, fearful that Grandpa knew his secret all along and was simply waiting for the opportune moment to teach him a lesson.

"No." Grandpa motioned. "What's on the rock?"

Willy squinted under the moonlight to focus in on the odd coloration siding the baseball sized stone. It was dark and thick, the flashlight's sparkle exposed a slight but notable hue of rouge that was familiar. The memory came upon him, swiftly and suddenly — blood squirting from the tick's bottom staining the stone step. That was the color. That's what was on the stone. Willy's eyes shot up at Grandpa in a whirlwind of confusion, but he said nothing.

"Do you know what it is?" Grandpa said a bit louder.

Willy shrugged. "Blood?"

Grandpa turned around. "This way..."

Grandpa began walking towards the house, though not the way they came, but in the same direction. Grandpa's steps slowed as the moon seemed to glow a bit brighter. Willy's throwing arm began to quiver. Grandpa stopped walking.

Grandpa's eyes shifted to where he held the light and as Willy approached so did his. He wasn't sure what he was seeing at first, oddly shaped nubs, but the closer he found himself, the clearer they became. Paws.

Willy stepped beside Grandpa and could see all that he saw; they had found Dog. Dog looked as though he'd been there for such a long time. Willy first saw it as his eyes ran up and down the still animal, the same rouge he had seen the rock and on the stone step. But this hue was near the top of Dog's head, just above his left eye, and there was much more. The hue had dried, settled. It had dripped down Dog's face and fallen to the outer ring of his collar. His eyes were open; Willy saw the moonlight's reflection in them.

"I told you to stop throwing those rocks, Willy," Grandpa whispered.

Willy felt the jolt that would occupy his arm and shoulder shift to his stomach as the weight of the rocks suddenly became too heavy for him to carry. His knees began to tremble as a gust of wind blew a horrid scent in his direction. He cringed as the aroma crept up his nose, travelling to the back of his throat where he tasted it, forcing him to gag. Willy tried to speak, but the words got stuck.

"You should have listened to me," Grandpa spoke firmly.

"I-" Willy's voice shook, "I di-"

"This didn't have to happen," Grandpa interrupted.

The lie flew out before Willy could catch it. "But I did stop."

Grandpa's eyes widened as Willy's transparency mutated to the time the old man found inexplicably difficult to bury, even after 40 years, to the time he sipped on anything that would blur the memory of the ex-wife that told him he'd never amount to more than a worthless weed farmer, to the time half his platoon charged onto a landmine before a cloud of orange and brown burst from the dirt and their limbs fell with the rain, to the time he was fired from his second job for having booze on his breath during a scheduled inspection, to the time he begged his sister to take out a third loan on the farm he secretly mortgaged ten years earlier, to the time he thought of nothing more than rubbing bottles between his fingers and swallowing the harsh potency that made everything seem alright, to the time he came home drunk after ten hours of nothing but cheap bar beers and picked up his baby girl before tripping over the coffee table, sending her head first into the solid oak floor he helped his father sand as a boy, to the lie he told his wife when she asked him about the bruise on the child's head the next morning as he watched her eyes widen at his flagrant lie and she seemed to sing "it has to stop."

Grandpa looked down at the lifeless dog then back at his grandson.

"I told you it was dangerous!" Grandpa yelled so fiercely Willy stumbled back.

His voiced echoed far off into the field as the world suddenly became still. The wheat froze when Grandpa screamed — like it had never heard him scream before; it was as still as Willy had ever seen it. Its stalks straightened, stiffened up, afraid to move, and the wind's howl became lost in the sound's remnants. It was scared, the wheat; it was scared of Grandpa. Willy looked into the shadows occupying Grandpa's face, but could not see the small tear forming in his left eye. They stood for a moment, over Dog. They stood and watched each other in the darkness. They watched the faces they could not see clearly and listened to the wind they could no longer hear.

Grandpa rubbed between his eyes and handed Willy the light. "Take this and go back to bed."

Willy tried to speak, "But–"

"Just go." Grandpa gently pushed the light into Willy's stomach.

Willy started walking home but peered over

his shoulder. He saw Grandpa bend down, rub his hand over Dog's resting body, then pick him up and carry him further into the field. Then, Willy could no longer see them.

Willy lay in bed for hours, unable to sleep. Every time he closed his eyes he imagined Dog's paws, the rouge hue settled in his fur, and the stunning stillness of the moon in his eye. He thought about what he said to Grandpa, that he had stopped throwing stones, and under the pale blue sheets Willy shut his eyes and wished the lie had been the truth. He wished and wished that it had been the truth, wished and wished it wasn't a lie, wished until he fell asleep as the sky grew bright and shifted into a subtle shade of orange.

Breakfast was quiet the next morning. Grandpa finished his food and grabbed a crossword then sat out on the back porch. Willy took a few more bites and before he realized it, was standing on the porch next to Grandpa. He didn't remember debating whether or not to follow him outside, or clearing his and Grandpa's plates from the table, or shoving his hands in his pockets as he tried to find the words that got stuck the night before.

"Grandpa," Willy said softly.

"Hmm," Grandpa mumbled, barely looking up from his crossword.

"Where'd you take Dog?"

Grandpa's hand became still and he glanced at Willy. "To other side of the field."

"To bury him?" Willy asked.

Grandpa nodded. Willy sat in the chair next to him and looked out onto the wheat field as it bent in the breeze.

"Grandpa," Willy said. "I didn't really stop throwin-"

"I know." Grandpa interrupted before looking back down at his crossword.

Willy felt the weight of the stones again, as if trapped at the bottom of the divot covered by them. His heart began thudding and his throat became moist; he felt his eyes beginning to water as the stuck words loosened.

"Grandpa," Willy said in a whisper. "I didn't mean to hurt him."

Grandpa closed his book. "You did a little more than hurt him, Willy."

Willy closed his eyes, attempting to keep the water from running free, when he felt Grandpa's long fingers wrap around his shoulder again. Willy looked up as that water came out anyway.

Grandpa asked him, "You sorry, boy?"

Willy nodded as Grandpa placed his hand over his wet cheek, covering the entire side of Willy's face, and used his thumb to wipe away the boy's tears.

"Okay then," Grandpa said with a slow nod before he let go. "Go on inside and get packed for tomorrow."

But Willy did not move. He didn't lean forward, steady his elbows to push off the arms of the chair, or attempt the slightest bend of knee; instead, he watched the wheat unbend as the wind took halt and a warm dusting surrounded him and his grandfather.

"Is being sorry enough, Grandpa?" Willy asked. "It won't bring him back."

"I suppose," Grandpa hesitated. "That's why it has to be."

Grandpa looked at Willy, Willy back at him, and the two sat as silent as they did the night before. They watched the faces they suddenly saw clearly, and stared into a familiar darkness. Willy's gaze shifted towards the wheat field as he and Grandpa continued in their silence, and he thought of something. Not the smell of oranges or Old Spice, not the sound of Grandma's knitting needles and Grandpa's pencil against the crossword, not Dog lying dead in the field or the way the weight of the stones touched him when he thought of not being able to tell him just how sorry he was, he didn't even think about the bloody stone hidden amongst the rows of frightened wheat. Instead, Willy thought about that painting, that beautiful stupid painting of a boy leaning against a big unrecognizable tree sitting 15 feet above the riverbank, fishing for stones.

The Abada

*Lester first met his lifelong companion on the sec-
ond day of the first grade,* just after a game of ring
around. The students held hands and assumed
the necessary circle, when Lester put his hand out
for his classmate, Amelia, to take hold of. Instead
of grabbing Lester's hand, Ameila pulled away
and stared at it. She stared long and hard. This
confused Lester, so he began staring, too. Four
fingers, one thumb—Lester recalled being told a
thumb was not the same as a finger—five nails,
five knuckles, and a palm; yeah, everything was
there. So, he glanced at Amelia's hand—four fingers, one thumb, five nails, five knuckles, and a
palm, the same things he had.

"I don't want to hold hands with you," Amelia
said.

For a moment, a small piece of Lester wanted

to ask Amelia why she didn't want to, but it was only for a moment, and only a small piece. Lester balled his extended hand into a fist and retracted the way Amelia had.

"Well, I don't want to hold your hand, either," he said before walking off.

He sat far enough away to be on his own. Lester looked at his hand again, and heard a voice whisper from behind.

"It was nothing you did, you know."

Lester turned around and saw a thing he'd never seen before, about his height and shaped like a thick, miniature horse. Its coat was coal black and smooth, reflecting the sun off its solid back. It resembled a unicorn but had two horns instead of one— two gray, not silver, twisted horns, one that pointed up and another that pointed down. Its eyes were so big and brown that Lester could swear he saw the whole world in them. It was the most beautiful thing he had ever seen.

"Who are you?" Lester asked.

"Your Abada," the Abada replied.

"That's your name?"

"No," the Abada said, "That is what I am. I have no name."

"Why not?"

"Because it is simply the way it is," the Abada

took a seat next to Lester.

"What did you mean when you said it was nothing I did?"

The Abada motioned to Lester's classmates, "When the girl did not take your hand, it was not your fault. It was because she saw me."

Lester's eye widened, "You mean everyone can see you?"

"No," the Abada explained. "Not everyone."

"Which ones?" Lester insisted.

"Just the ones that choose to," the Abada replied.

"But why did Amelia treat you like that, you're so cool!"

The Abada looked directly at Lester and said, "I don't look like her."

"So," Lester said, confused.

"So," the Abada echoed. "For her, that is enough."

Lester paused before he said, "Okay, let's find Trevor, I want to tell him about yo—"

"You cannot," the Abada interrupted, "You can only tell some about me once you are sure they have an Abada as well."

Lester frowned, "Will Trevor get one? He's my best friend, I tell him everything."

"He will," the Abada affirmed.

Lester hesitated, "Will Amelia?"

The Abada shook his head.

Lester stood and started for the playground before turning around and looking back at his Abada, "You're not going to leave, are you? You'll really stay forever?"

The Abada smiled again and said, "Always."

Lester and the Abada grew, and in a few years the Abada was bigger Lester.

"I think you're getting *too* big," Lester stressed. "More people are noticing you, they look longer, stare harder."

"You'll grow accustomed to it," the Abada replied. "Your book bag is big and heavy, right? You carry it with you every day…"

"But if my bag gets too heavy, I can move it to the other shoulder, or put it down for a few minutes."

"You will learn to adjust to me too, Lester," the Abada said.

Lester later caught up with Trevor at lunch.

"What's up, Trev?" Lester asked.

"I hate school," he replied.

"Why?"

"Because everything is so boring. We stare at numbers an—"

"I like numbers," Lester interrupted.

"I know," Trevor went on. "I guess they're okay... But then we go to social studies and read about everybody else's problems, then to history to study everybody else's wars, and finally to English, where we listen to stories about things that don't really happen. Not to me and you, anyway. It's just so boring. I had to go to the guidance office, so the counsellor could help me get my grades up."

"What did he tell you?"

"To join a sports team, said it might help me focus," Trevor cleared his throat and pretended to adjust an invisible pair of glasses, "He goes; *you'd probably excel at sports, why not give basketball a try?*"

Lester rolled his eyes.

Trevor whispered, "My 'you-know-what' said I should get used to it. Said the people that see him see strong legs and big muscles... good for sports..."

"You are pretty fast," Lester said, with a smirk.

"Of course I am," Trevor grinned. "I have an Abada!"

The boys laughed. Lester went to Trevor's house after school. They finished their homework, grabbed a snack, and played catch.

They lost track of time when Lester's Abada chimed in, "It is getting late, Lester. You know you are supposed to be home before dark."

Lester looked out the window and saw the red sky, his body became still, but only for a moment. He knew what happened to the Abada after dark, and he couldn't believe he was cutting it this close. Lester grabbed his bag and waved to Trevor. It wasn't a long walk home, but it seemed like twilight was running up on them. Lester got nervous.

"Do you think we'll make it?" Lester asked.

"You should not have put us in this situation," the Abada snapped.

Lester's voice shook, "I'm sorry, I didn't realiz—"

"Save it," the Abada interrupted. "You think a *sorry* will help you if the wrong person sees me? You know what happens, Lester!"

Lester picked up the pace, his brisk walk morphed into a jog as the sky darkened and the night breeze set in.

"I get bigger at night, my eyes turn red, mane turns to fire, and my horns grow four times their size. If someone sees me at night, it is not safe for you, Lester."

Lester sped up again and his eyes began to water.

He adjusted his book bag and said, "I don't understand why it's so bad at night, you don't look any different to me."

"It is always bad, but night offers the cloak I warned you about," the Abada started moving faster as Lester's jog became a light run. The Abada continued, "The cloak of excuses, of their reasons—"

"I know, I know," Lester cut in. "I remember."

The light run was a full out sprint by then, Lester and the Abada felt their hearts thrashing as their soles clapped the pavement around the corner from Lester's house.

"We made it," Lester shouted then slowed as he saw his home in the distance.

The Abada did not slow down, Lester caught up and the two ran a few more feet, making it in just before nightfall. Both caught their breath, but the Abada paced the floor, unable to calm down.

"Do not do that again, Lester. Do not ever put us in that situation, again. Not if you do not have to, not if you do not have to," the Abada seemed to sing.

Lester approached his companion and took hold of his face. He rested his forehead between the Abada's eyes and felt his horns against his cheeks, they were cold and wet, like the Abada had been crying. The two stood quietly, watching each other watch each other.

Lester spoke, "Your eyes aren't red and your mane isn't fire, your horns are no bigger and neither are you, you are the same. Your eyes will never look red, to me."

The Abada rubbed his head against Lester's, thankful for his young friend, and after a few more breaths, finally felt safe. Lester didn't lie to the Abada about the color of his eyes; he saw no red and never would. But the world he once saw in the Abada's eyes appeared smaller that night, much smaller. It was the only secret Lester never told him, and never would.

The school year started, and the boys mourned summer; Lester, not so much. There was something magnetic about the classroom — about the smell of chalkboards, exploration of science projects, and perseverance in math problems. There had been a big a change in his life over the summer, his Abada had grown to full size.

Lester and Trevor had become accustomed to the attention brought on by their companions, but it didn't make it much easier. They were heading to a bus stop after one of Trevor's away games. He decided to play basketball, after all. They didn't know the area well, but knew how to get to the stop. They had a good three hours before sunset.

"You remember the couple from last week?" Trevor asked.

"Which one?"

"Outside the mall, remember? The two going to their car after my mom dropped us off," Trevor explained.

"Oh," Lester recalled.

"You see how tight she grabbed his arm when we walked by, and the way he squeezed the bag..."

Lester sighed, "Who knows Trev? Maybe she just felt like holding his arm."

Trevor waited for a sarcastic slight to follow, but Lester didn't say anything else.

Trevor eyed his friend before saying, "And the bag?"

Lester shrugged, "I know. It's just annoying sometimes."

"People that do that sort of thing always are."

"No," Lester explained. "I mean, deciphering everything. Wondering if people are reacting to the Abadas or just reacting, looking at us or seeing them. I was walking to school last week, and some old lady was walking her dog. As soon as she saw me she started walking faster, I tried to ignore it, but couldn't. And I'm not crazy or making it up. We can imagine there's some other reason, but would people be peeking over their shoulder, clutching arms and bags if we didn't have Abadas?"

Before Trevor got the opportunity to respond, the boys heard the sirens directly behind them. The officers pulled up beside the boys and the one in the passenger seat rolled down his window.

"Afternoon, fellas," the officer said.

Trevor bit his lip as Lester responded, "Hi."

"Don't think I've seen you two around here before," he said.

Lester became tense. He felt Trevor's body become still next to him, like a statue, he didn't think he'd ever heard Trevor so quiet. Lester's Abada wasn't though, he kept whispering the same two phrases as he stood next to Lester, *the cloak*, and *do not give them a reason*. It was as if time had slowed to Lester, and the words rang with a continuous echo, *the cloak, do not give them a reason, the cloak, do not give them a reason*.

Lester said, "No, we were at the high school for his basketball game."

He motioned to Trevor.

The officer's eyes cut towards Trevor, "You play?"

Trevor nodded as he began reaching for the jersey hanging outside his gym bag.

"Hey," the officer shouted, startling both boys. "What are you doing?"

Trevor showed the officer his palms, "Nothing."

The officer opened his door, "Drop the bag."

Trevor looked at Lester and the cop repeated, "I said drop the bag!"

The officer reached for something on his belt, he didn't take it out, just kept his hand on it. Lester could hear Trevor's heart beating louder than he could hear his own. He watched Trevor slide the bag off his shoulder as the cop in the driver's seat started to get out of the car.

"Walk this way," the officer finger directed Trevor before looking at Lester. "And you, sit on the curb with your hands where I can see them."

Lester sat, hands high, as Trevor approached the officer.

"Spread your legs and put your hands on the vehicle," the officer said before the pat down began. "Do you have anything on you that could poke me?"

"No," Trevor's voice shook.

Lester watched from the ground as the cop's hands pressed along Trevor's legs. As they gripped his thighs and hipbone, ran across his back and shoulders, reached around and caressed his torso, as they cupped his massive wingspan. Lester watched as his friend shuttered in place, the same fluid limbs he just watched sway across hardwood, dance through defenders, and soar amongst the ceiling, rigid, stiff, and shaking. Lester watched his friend and desperately wanted to tell him everything was going to be alright but couldn't.

"Check the bag," the officer said to the other cop before looking at Trevor. "What were you reaching for?"

"I was going to show you my jersey," Trevor whispered so low Lester barely heard.

"For what?" The officer asked.

"You asked me if I played ball..."

The cop dug around for a few more seconds, searching, then stood up and walked over to his partner.

The officer clapped his hand on Trevor's back, "Alright, you fellas get home safe."

Neither responded. Lester lowered his hands and stood, Trevor grabbed his bag and they went to the bus stop. The entire wait was silent, as was most of the bus ride, until Lester finally spoke.

Lester looked at Trevor. "You good man, that was craz—"

Trevor blew.

"What?"

Trevor said, "Who knows, Les, maybe they were just doing their jobs."

Lester shook his head, "Why'd they even stop —"

Lester stopped himself when he realized just how stupid the question sounded.

"Because of a friggin' jersey," Trevor crossed his arms.

Lester's stop came and he said bye to his friend. He got home and went directly to where the photo albums were. He flipped through a few pages and stopped at his kindergarten class photo. Lester rubbed his thumb against his four-year-old face and tried to remember that time. He tried and tried, but everything was a blur. He so badly wanted to remember what it was like back then, before growing up, before meeting his companion, before anything. He rubbed his young face as two small splashes bounced against the plastic and slowly dragged to the bottom of the book. Lester touched his face but knew they weren't his tears. They belonged to the being hovering above him, looking down at the picture of the boy he never had a chance to meet.

Lester was furious, walking home from his seventh interview the summer before his last year of high school.

"I'm telling you Trev? There's no point!" Lester said into his cellphone. "I need more experience for college applications, but the only places that will hire me to tutor are recs and community centers."

"Keep applying," Trevor said. "Someone will get back to you, Les."

They hung up and Lester's thoughts trickled back to the interview he just came from.

"Trevor is right, you know," the Abada said. "Someone will get back to you."

Lester let out an exaggerated exhale as the Abada went on, "If you persevere, success will always come."

Lester thought about the interview. *Do you have any experience outside city centers?* How could he if no one would hire him.

"It will get easier, Lester," the Abada continued.

Lester tuned the Abada out. *What about experience tutoring…* the interviewer paused, Lester saw her searching for the right word, *suburban youth?*

"Lester," the Abada said. "Are you listening to me?"

"What!" Lester's shouted. "What do you want?"

"I am just trying to talk to you," the Abada's voice lowered.

Lester threw his hands up, "I don't always feel like talking! Can't you just leave me alone for a while?"

"You know I cannot do that, Lester," the Abada said.

"Yeah..." Lester began walking towards the pier. "Tell me something, are you the reason no one will hire me?"

The Abada shrugged, "Maybe, I am not sure wha—"

"Well, what are you sure of then?" Lester snapped, "Except for the fact that I can't get rid you. I have the experience and references, and still, nothing... I know it's because of you."

The Abada replied as they approached the shore, "No one said things were going to be easy."

Lester stopped walking, "It's because you're hanging over my shoulder and scaring the shit out of everyone—just give me some space."

"Not everyone."

Lester rolled his eyes and walked away. Each step he took over the wet sand slowed him a bit, but his strides were long. The Abada found himself rushing to keep up.

Lester mumbled, "Stop following me."

The Abada just kept on behind his companion and said nothing.

"STOP!" Lester yelled as he continued to march.

The Abada said nothing, only followed at a distance.

Lester stopped then, picked up a handful of small pebbles, and glared at the Abada.

"Just leave me alone," Lester gripped one of the pebbles. "Go away..."

Lester and the Abada stood parallel to each other, some few feet away. The tide had picked up and all they heard was the water. Its sloshing tendency, that coming and going way it would take to just before sunset. It was rushing towards them, foamy and strong, the water smelled of dirt. The pier was empty, it almost never was, but it was barren that day so no one could see them. The world was still and quiet; only Lester holding the stone, waiting to see what the Abada would say.

"I cannot," the Abada whispered, but not quiet enough for Lester not to hear.

Lester exhaled and pulled his arm back. He shifted the pebble between his thumb and pointer finger, tightened his wrist, took aim directly at the Abada's body, and then released. The stone hit the Abada in his chest. The Abada stumbled back, not from pain, but from the shock. Lester placed another stone in his right hand.

"Go away."

The Abada only shook his head.

So Lester threw another, and another, each snap the wrist more assertive then the last. The Abada winced as the stones pierced his hide. Once Lester was finished with the hand full, he grabbed another, and another, and he whipped those rocks one after another. Some small, some not so small, he continued to hurl the stones at his Abada until he was exhausted, until he had to sit in the sand with his head between his legs.

"Just leave me alone," Lester said under his breath.

The Abada, sore from the beating, joined Lester and sat beside him, "I just wanted to make sure you were oka—"

"What about what I want?" Lester looked at his bruised friend. "I don't want to have to worry about you all the time. I just want to know that if I'm not hired somewhere it's because someone was more qualified, not because of you. I just..."

Lester hesitated, letting the mist from the tide sprinkle over his face, "I just want to be Lester. Not Lester and the Abada, you know?"

The Abada nodded, "I know. I wish that we did not live in a world with Abadas and others like us. But we do, Lester, and I sometimes think we always will."

Lester wiped his face, "It's just so hard, sometimes."

Lester leaned his head against the Abada and put his hand over one of his sore spots, "I'm sorry."

"Ahh," the Abada grinned. "Things get thrown at me all the time, Lester. I wish they were all as tiny as sand stones."

Lester smiled and looked upon the greatness of his Abada as the tide came in and the water ran across his feet in all its dirt-ridden, foamy strength.

The following year Trevor received a full athletic scholarship to university, but first had to attend a junior college to lift his grades. Lester got accepted into a school just outside the city. He decided to major in education with a mathematics concentration. He remembered wishing there was someone that might be able to better understand Trevor's boredom in school.

Lester compared the first few months at school to a sitcom he used to watch, "it *is* a *Different World*." He later realized it wasn't so different, just a smaller version. The same supposition that he was on some sports team, or that he was looking for directions when he entered the mathematics building, or that he must have been thrilled when the cafeteria served fried chicken, or that his roommate was shocked when he heard him listening to Coldplay; it wasn't such a different world.

Lester was in touch with Trevor once a week, and Trev was having a blast. He was the superstar. Loved by all, averaging twenty-four points, nine rebounds a night—the superstar. That's why Lester was so caught off guard.

Lester answered his cell as the operator stated, "This call will be recorded and monitored. You have a collect call from an inmate..."

Lester froze. He recognized Trevor's voice on the other end, but how could it be.

He frowned as the operator concluded, "Will you accept the charges?"

"Yes," Lester replied.

There was a soft and short clicking sound.

"Hey, Les," Trevor whispered.

"What the hell is going on?" Lester raised his voice, "What are you doing in jail?"

Trevor began, "It's because of some dumb shit, Les. Me and a couple of the guys went to this party after the game Saturday. We were chillin', and everything was cool until some guys we just played came in and started hyping up. Things got heated, man. Next thing we know five-0 pulls up, and I'm in the back of a cop car."

"So, what," Lester asked. "You were charged with assault?"

"Yeah, and resisting arrest."

Lester eyes widened before he covered his face, "What the fuck, Trevor?"

Trevor hesitated.

"I know, man" Trevor whispered. "But, hell if I was going to let what happened to me before happen again."

"What happened to us," Lester corrected him.

"No," Trevor said. "It happened to me, Les. You just sat on the damn side walk."

Both became quiet.

"I'm nobody's bitch." Trevor snapped. "They weren't going to put their hands all over me again, Les."

"You can't do that shit bro, they'll kill you."

"Well," Trevor concluded. "I ain't dead yet."

Lester hit his head against the wall before saying, "I got to go."

"Okay," Trevor said. "Can I call you tomorrow?"

Lester nodded, "Yeah, be safe."

They hung up. Lester stared at the beige wall of

his dorm room and imagined Trevor staring at the gray bricks around him; both dull, bleak shades, both awaiting a spark of color. Lester couldn't paint his wall, but he could cover it with a poster, some pictures or postcards. Trevor didn't have that luxury anymore, and the thought angered Lester.

"How could he do this?" Lester asked his Abada.

The Abada replied, "The same way anyone could."

"He's going to lose his scholarship," Lester said. "We're never given anything, and he just threw it all away."

"Did he?" the Abada questioned.

And suddenly, Lester wasn't sure. He wasn't sure about anything.

Trevor was charged with misdemeanor assault two months later, and was ordered to serve nine months in a state penitentiary. With time already served, he'd have six months to complete. Trevor never talked about prison. Not one time in the hundreds of calls he made to Lester. So Lester never asked him about it. They talked about Lester mostly. How he was doing in school and bits of pop-culture. Lester would always tell him the time would fly by, but it didn't seem to. It was the longest nine months of their lives. Trevor lost his scholarship, but got the opportunity to play in a semi-pro league after his release. He called Lester from a bus near the Appalachian Mountains one early morning while the rest of his teammates slept.

"It's so beautiful here, Les," Trevor whispered. "Even at night, it's so damn beautiful."

Lester nodded. Forgetting his friends couldn't see him.

"I bet it is," he replied.

"Lester," Lester swore he heard Trevor's heart beating through the phone, as loud as it was all those years ago the first time he heard it. "I'm one of the lucky ones, aren't I?"

Lester exhaled and he heard his own heart beating then. He never did answer Trevor's question. Instead, Lester looked up at his Abada, silent and settled, looking down at the now man he'd stand with for the rest of their lives. Its eyes were still so full and so brown, and even though he didn't see the whole world in them anymore, they were still the most beautiful thing Lester had ever seen.

Portrait by Mae Chen 陈美

Morgan Christie's work has appeared in *Room, Aethlon, Moko, Little Patuxent Review, Obra/Artifact, Blackberry: A Magazine,* and has been anthologized in BLF Press's *Black to the Future.* Her poetry chapbook, *Variations on a Lobster's Tale,* was the winner of the 2017 Alexander Posey Chapbook Prize (University of Central Oklahoma Press, 2018) and her second poetry chapbook, *Sterling,* was released in 2019 (CW Books, 2019). She was the winner of the 2018 Likely Red Fiction Chapbook contest and has been nominated for a Pushcart Prize and Best of the Net.

CPSIA information can be obtained
at www.ICGtesting.com
Printed in the USA
FSHW011124031120
75401FS